KING TIDE

A Southern Outer Banks Novel

BOBBY BRYAN GOODWIN

Core Sound Media LLC

First Edition

eBook ISBN: 978-1-971-321-00-4
Paperback ISBN: 978-1-971-321-01-1
Hardcover ISBN: 978-1-971-321-02-8

Printed in the United States of America

Published by Core Sound Media, LLC
www.coresoundmedia.com

For those who came before us
and the generations yet to come.

Contents

Chapter One

The Ferry

He was rowing. That was all he knew. Oars biting into black water, cold spray stinging his face, voices shouting a name that might have been his. The boat heaved beneath him. Somewhere ahead, a woman's pale hand reached through splintered wood—

The ferry horn shattered the dream.

Deep. Resonant. A vibration that rolled across the water and through the steel structures of the Cedar Island terminal, stirring the heaviest sleepers inside their vehicles.

Inside a weathered pickup truck at the front of the line, Jesse Dixon startled awake. The horn's call pressed through the fogged windows, pulling him from the remnants of the dream into this gray coastal dawn. For a moment, he couldn't remember where he was—only that the air smelled different. Salt instead of pine. Diesel instead of wood smoke.

His heart was still racing—oars, black water, a hand reaching. He knew he had lived that dream before. It was one of those dreams that kept resurfacing.

He rubbed his face, felt the stubble he hadn't bothered to shave before they'd left. His reflection in the rearview was a blur—dark brown hair flattened on one side, shadows under eyes that usually carried more confidence than he felt. Wiry frame, his mother always said. Built for rivers, not football fields.

His grandfather's cabin flickered through his half-sleep—the way morning light fell through hemlock branches onto the porch where he'd learned to tie flies at seven years old. That smell of woodsmoke and coffee. Gone now, the cabin sold, the land subdivided. Some things you only get to keep in your chest.

He blinked into the dimness. The windshield was opaque with condensation, the world beyond it erased by fog. Sadie curled in the passenger seat beside him, hoodie pulled over her face, one hand resting on Scout's fur.

Behind closed eyes, she was somewhere else—the French Broad in late spring, water high and fast, Jesse's voice calling out the line as they dropped into a rapid. The canoe bucking beneath her. Boone whooping from the stern. Cold spray on her face, and the last thing she remembered saying before the horn pulled her awake: Nothing can stop us.

The yellow Lab mix slept curled in the footwell, chest rising and falling in slow waves. Boone sprawled across the backseat at impossible angles, long legs tangled in discarded jackets.

Before dawn had fully broken over Cedar Island, the world lingered in that delicate hush between the last breath of night and the first whisper of morning. Fog slid across Pamlico Sound in slow, unhurried ribbons, drifting over the asphalt and curling around pilings as though the island itself were stretching awake beneath a gray blanket. Through the moisture-thick air, amber terminal lights glowed like lanterns half-sunk in a dream, revealing trucks and trailers and early risers only in fragments.

Jesse wiped condensation from the glass with his sleeve. Out there, somewhere in the haze, the Sound moved with a slow, unbothered rhythm—gentle laps of water against wooden pilings that came and went like the breathing of something enormous and unseen.

Their truck sat loaded with gear from the mountains—a johnboat and canoe strapped to the roof and bed, their hulls scraped from riverbeds far from the coast. Knotted ropes curled across coolers and dry bags. No motors. Just paddles and oars strapped alongside—the way they'd always preferred it.

Three summers on the Nantahala. Two on the French Broad. One ill-advised overnight on the Chattooga that none of them talked about but all of them remembered whenever rain hit a tent fly. The gear told the story of who they were together.

A sharp knock hit the driver's window.

The sudden sound sliced through the quiet interior like the snap of a branch in a dark forest. Scout was on her feet instantly, nails scraping the floor mat as a low growl rumbled in her chest. Jesse jerked more fully awake, settling into something steadier but alert. Sadie blinked into the dimness, pulling the hoodie off her face as shapes outside began to assemble into something human.

A ferry worker's face emerged from the amber light, features blurred at the edges.

Middle-aged, with a thick red beard and a Down East accent worn as naturally as his vest.

His reflective vest glowed faintly, droplets of moisture collecting on its fabric as he leaned closer to the window.

"Mornin'. Got a reservation? And I need to see an ID."

Jesse's voice cracked with sleep as he answered, his fingers fumbling briefly toward his wallet. The windows still held the night's chill, and his breath formed a faint mist on the glass as he leaned closer. "Yes sir... under Dixon."

"What time is it?" Sadie muttered, rubbing her eyes with the heel of her hand.

"Time to board the ferry," the worker smirked, tapping the side of the truck with two knuckles before stepping back into the fog.

Boone groaned from the backseat, shifting himself upright with exaggerated effort.

He squinted at the fog, then at Jesse. "Tell me again why we couldn't take a trip somewhere with, I don't know, actual roads? Maybe a Waffle House?"

He unfolded himself from the backseat—taller than Jesse, broader through the shoulders, four years hauling lumber and framing houses. Smart in ways that had nothing to do with classrooms.

His phone sat dark in his pocket. Three days now since he'd texted her back. He wasn't ready to explain why.

"Man, they act like we're boarding a cruise ship."

"Just doin' his job, Boone," Jesse murmured, though a sleepy smile tugged at the corner of his mouth. Scout settled again, head between her paws but ears twitching as the worker moved on.

They pulled forward, the truck rolling slowly as headlights carved narrow tunnels through the fog. The beams fractured on droplets in the air, drifting shards of light that swirled like the dust of some waking dream. The ramp ahead rose from the mist like a piece of old machinery forgotten by time—steel grating wet with condensation, rails slick and dark, the Sound murmuring below.

As the tires clanged over the ramp, vibrations thrummed up through the truck's frame. Jesse felt them in his ribs, a reminder of metal meeting metal, of motion shifting from land to water. Boone pressed a hand to the ceiling as if steadying himself, though the ferry had barely begun to accept them.

Halfway up, a silhouette formed through the fog—broad-shouldered, still as a piling, but with an easy familiarity to the deck beneath him.

Caleb O'Neal stood waiting, waving them aboard.

Tall, sun-worn, blond hair catching what little early light existed. He looked like someone the wind itself had shaped—steadfast, patient, at ease with the tide's moods. His deckhand uniform clung to him with the casual naturalness of someone who didn't just work on the water, but belonged to it. The fog curled around him, parting as though it knew him.

Sadie noticed immediately. Her posture lifted, a spark kindling behind her sleep-blurred eyes. "Okay... that deckhand is fine. Someone should've told me the ferry came with scenery already on board."

Boone stiffened beside Jesse, rolling his shoulders with a sharp exhale.

Jesse said nothing. He'd seen Boone react this way since they were kids—anytime some guy caught Sadie's attention. Protective. Territorial. Predictable. Jesse had learned long ago to let it pass without comment.

But something else nagged at him. Something about the way that deckhand stood there, easy and confident, like he belonged to this place in a way they never would. The way Sadie's eyes had lingered a second too long.

Jesse pushed the thought down and parked the truck. Boone could handle his own feelings. Jesse would handle his.

He'd been handling them for years. Since the summer before college, when she'd fallen asleep against his shoulder on his grandfather's porch and he'd stayed perfectly still for two hours rather than wake her. He'd known then. He just hadn't known what to do about it.

Jesse nearly laughed, biting back the sound as he cut the engine.

The moment the doors opened, the air wrapped around them—rich with brine, diesel, damp rope, and rusted metal. Scout hopped out eagerly, nails clicking across the ferry deck, tail wagging in curious sweeps as she trotted ahead, snuffling the smells of rope, salt, and the oily tang of machinery warming to life.

The ferry hummed beneath them, engines low and steady. The fog shifted lazily across the bow, revealing slivers of the Sound. The muted morning light gave everything a soft edge, as if the world were still deciding what kind of day it wanted to be.

Scout trotted ahead, but Sadie lingered by the truck, stretching. Her back cracked. She winced, then laughed.

"Six hours in a truck will do that," Jesse said, moving beside her.

"Worth it though." She tilted her head back, breathing in the salt air. When she opened her eyes, Jesse was already looking out at the water, profile sharp against the gray morning.

She studied him for a moment—the way he always went quiet when he was working through something. She'd seen that look a thousand times growing up. On riverbanks. Around campfires. Late nights on his porch when they were supposed to be studying.

"You okay?" she asked.

He glanced at her, and for a moment he was back on his grandfather's porch, her head on his shoulder, the smell of woodsmoke in her hair. "Yeah. Just glad you're here."

"Where else would I be?" She bumped his shoulder with hers as they walked toward the rail. "You'd get lost without me."

"Probably true."

"Definitely true. Remember that time you tried to read a map upside down for nearly an hour?"

"That was one time," Jesse protested, but he was grinning now.

"One very memorable time."

She reached over and straightened his collar where it had folded wrong in his sleep—an automatic gesture, the kind that comes from years of proximity. He let her.

Scout circled back, tail wagging, and nosed between them as they reached the bow. Sadie rested her hand on the rail near Jesse's—not touching, but close enough to feel the warmth.

Boone followed with reluctant steps, hands in his hoodie pockets. At the bow, the fog parted just enough to show layers of gray-blue stretching across the water, the horizon vanishing and reappearing as if breathing.

Jesse leaned against the rail, inhaling the sharp salt air. "Sun's coming up. Pretty time."

Scout pressed against Jesse's leg. Her head swiveled, nostrils flaring as she catalogued everything: the diesel exhaust from the ferry's engines, sharp and oily; the salt spray coming off the Sound; the fish smell clinging to ropes and deck planks; another dog somewhere onboard, its scent mixing with the vinyl and coffee smells drifting from the parked vehicles. Her tail wagged faster.

Jesse rested his hand on her head, feeling her body quiver with the effort to process it all. Every smell told a story she was trying to read.

"She's going crazy," Sadie said, watching Scout's nose twitch.

"Everything's new," Jesse said. "Back home it's hardwoods, creek water, and deer. Here it's—"

"Fish and boats and seagulls," Sadie finished, laughing as Scout pulled toward the rail, desperate to get closer to whatever she was smelling.

Sadie stepped beside him, fingers brushing the cold metal. "Was it like this last time you were here?"

The hull's steady rhythm against the water felt as old as tides themselves. Jesse didn't answer immediately; he watched the Sound wake in its own slow rhythm, the haze rolling across it like breath from a slumbering giant. He swallowed, his chest rising with a quiet heaviness.

"It wasn't this pretty then," Jesse said, voice softening. "But it's the sound of the water splashing that I remember most. That sound... sounds like a waterfall back home in the mountains."

Sadie nodded, the corners of her eyes warming with the memory he offered her. "It really does."

He exhaled, grounding himself in the moment. "The last time I rode this ferry was right before college. Tryin' to figure out where I wanted to go. State or Carolina... We hung out that whole summer—you helped me make the list of pros and cons. Remember?"

"I remember."

She watched him more carefully now, sensing something shifting beneath the surface. The haze wrapped around them like a thin veil, the horizon fading in and out.

"Now that college is over... I'm hopin' this trip helps me figure things out again."

Sadie squeezed his hand. "Your dad called again, didn't he?"

Jesse exhaled through his nose. "Three times yesterday. About the teaching position in Raleigh."

The voicemails sat in his phone like stones. His father's voice in each one—calm, reasonable, disappointed in that quiet way that cut deeper than shouting ever could. They need your answer by Friday, Jesse. This isn't something you can paddle away from. As if Jesse didn't know that. As if running was all he'd ever done.

His father was ready to co-sign the apartment lease in Raleigh. If Jesse said no, he'd be saying no to more than a job. He'd be saying no to the only safety net he had left.

"And?"

"And I told him I'd think about it." He watched the water, jaw tight. "It's a good job. Good school. But it's the city, Sadie. Traffic and noise and... I don't know."

"You could go back to the mountains," Sadie offered quietly.

"I could. But that feels like moving backward, not forward." His voice dropped. "And then there's this." He gestured at the Sound, the fog lifting, the endless water. "I love it down here. The way it feels. The way it breathes different. But I don't know if that's real or if I'm just running from having to make a choice."

Sadie was quiet for a moment. He knew that silence—she was thinking, choosing her words carefully the way she always did.

"City, mountains, coast," Jesse said. "And I don't know which one could actually home. If any of them."

Sadie leaned closer, her shoulder brushing his. "We've all got things to figure out, Jesse. Maybe I'll figure some things out too... maybe we'll figure some things out together."

The words hung between them, a contrast to the cool wind tugging at her hoodie. Boone stepped up behind them with a grunt, his presence breaking the moment.

"View's over-rated."

Scout pushed her head against Sadie's leg as if disagreeing, the warmth of her fur grounding them in the present.

Footsteps approached along the deck—steady, sure, unhurried. The kind of stride that came from knowing the water better than the land.

"Pretty mornin' to cross."

Caleb approached with an easy gait, the last remnants of the fog curling away from him as though granting him passage. He paused a few steps from them, his posture relaxed, hands resting lightly on the railing.

"Some days the Sound's like a lamb... some days a lion. Today? She's a postcard."

"We'll take a postcard day," Jesse said, his breath misting faintly between words.

Scout trotted toward Caleb, tail wagging in a slow, hopeful arc. Caleb knelt, scratching behind her ears with a practiced gentleness. The dog leaned into him instantly, her body melting into his touch as if she'd known him for years.

Boone's expression tightened into something he didn't quite mask. Sadie's eyes lingered a heartbeat too long on Caleb's easy smile.

Sadie tilted her head, her hair catching a faint breeze. "Your accent... does everybody down here all talk like you do?"

"Some of us do," Caleb said with a grin. "Depends how long your folks been on the island."

"It almost sounds... Australian," Jesse said, studying him.

Caleb's laugh was short but warm. "Yeah, I hear that a lot. Ain't Australian, though. It's old stuff—Elizabethan English. Been spoken on these islands for over three hundred years. Way my granddaddy talked... and his before him."

Sadie's expression softened. "It sounds older. Kind of beautiful."

"We were raised on the water from the time we could walk," Caleb replied. "Some folks learn to talk from books. We learned from the tides. I'm Caleb. Caleb O'Neal from Ocracoke."

Jesse felt the words settle somewhere beneath his ribs. What would it be like to belong somewhere that completely?

"I'm Jesse Dixon and this is Sadie Whittaker. And this is our best friend Boone."

Caleb's gaze drifted toward their truck, taking in the boats strapped to the top. "Y'all ain't got no shortage of equipment."

"We're from the mountains," Sadie said. "Always outdoors. We like to be prepared."

Caleb lifted a brow, an amused tilt of curiosity. "Plannin' to paddle 'round the harbor?"

"Actually, planning to paddle over to Portsmouth Island," Jesse said. "I was over there four years ago, it's a special place."

Caleb's expression tightened subtly—his eyes narrowing by a fraction before he masked the reaction.

"It's special, alright. But it's farther than it looks. Wind, tide, current—might make it difficult. And we've got King Tides this week."

Sadie's stance lifted, her interest sharpening. Boone crossed his arms, his eyes darting between Caleb and Jesse as though weighing their confidence against the islander's warning.

"Last year 'round this same time..." Caleb continued, his voice lowering. "Couple folks tried to beat a storm comin' back from Portsmouth. Didn't make it. Storm caught 'em. Waves swamped 'em... drowned 'fore anyone could reach 'em."

Jesse's chest tightened. He knew what it meant to swamp—water rushing over the gunwales, the boat turning sluggish beneath you, that instant when you realize you're not paddling anymore. You're swimming.

Sadie's hand found Jesse's sleeve—not grabbing, just touching. Boone's jaw worked once, the skepticism in his posture flickering. Scout pressed harder against Jesse's leg, reading the shift in the air.

The Sound held its breath.

Sadie broke the silence, her voice thinner now. "Are you saying the passage to Portsmouth will be dangerous?"

"Not sayin' dangerous... on a purty day... if folks know what they're doin'," Caleb said. "But definitely a challenge... 'specially with the boats y'all got."

His eyes drifted briefly to Jesse, locking with a quiet, measured weight—one that carried warning, and respect, and something else Jesse couldn't quite name.

"Portsmouth's one of those places that draws people in," Caleb said. "Some say the veil's thin out there."

Jesse stopped mid-breath. A subtle hum filled his ears. The Sound seemed to hush, or maybe it was just something inside him.

"That's it," he said slowly. "That's the way the old village made me feel. Only place I've ever felt that."

He'd been seventeen, wandering alone through the abandoned village while his dad fished the inlet. The church with its empty pews. The cemetery where names had weathered to whispers. He had noticed his family name, Dixon, spread throughout the tombstones there. He'd stood in the doorway of an abandoned house and felt, for one breath, like someone was standing just behind him. Waiting. Watching.

"Whatever you felt there... I want to feel it too," Sadie said, voice low but sure.

Boone scoffed, shifting his weight as if shaking off the seriousness. "Veils, spirits... come on, man. It's an island, not a séance."

"Don't be an ass," Jesse said, but there was no heat in it. Just the practiced rhythm of friends who'd been needling each other for years.

"I'm not. I'm being a realist." Boone glanced at Caleb, then back at Jesse. "Portsmouth's what, three or four miles across open water? In a canoe? That's a long paddle when you've got tides working against you."

Caleb's expression shifted—something between respect and surprise. "You're right 'bout that."

"Rivers have current," Boone replied, "but the current never switches like tides do."

Caleb nodded slowly. "Exactly. River takes you one direction. Tide'll pull you in, pull you out, spin you sideways if you ain't payin' attention."

"We've paddled Class III rapids," Jesse said. "We can handle some open water."

"Different beast entirely," Caleb said, but there was respect in his voice now.

Boone had studied the tide charts before they'd left. Learned what a King Tide was. He did that—prepared quietly while everyone assumed he was just along for the ride.

A sudden flutter of wings filled the air, and a gull swooped overhead. Boone didn't notice until it was too late.

A wet splat landed directly on his shoulder.

Sadie gasped. Jesse choked back a laugh. Caleb's grin widened.

Boone's eyes widened with disbelief. "Oh come on—why are they targeting me today?"

Caleb let out a low chuckle. "Sound's got a sense of humor, ole boy."

"Boone's got an opinion about everything," Jesse added with a grin.

"Says the guy dragging us across open ocean to find himself." But Boone was almost smiling as he flicked at the mess with the edge of his sleeve.

Boone muttered curses under his breath while Sadie tried—and failed—not to laugh. Scout wagged her tail as if the whole thing was a game designed for her amusement.

Above them, Captain Riggs stepped out from the wheelhouse, leaning on the rail as he breathed in the softening fog. His weathered face angled toward the horizon. He'd listened to the weather radio earlier; today promised calm waters and a gentle wind—a good crossing. But he'd also noted a Nor'easter building out at sea, slow and steady. Men like him learned to respect the quiet signals long before the storm arrived.

His gaze slipped toward Caleb below. "Looks like Caleb's got his eye on 'nother one of them pretty tourist gals. Boy just cain't help himself," he chuckled under his breath.

Then his eyes shifted to the boats strapped to the truck. "If they gonna take them boats out... they best keep 'em close to shore," he murmured. "Good chance we gotta Nor'easter rollin' in a few days."

The ferry ride stretched into the morning as time seemed less and less relevant out here.

The ferry bumped lightly against the Ocracoke dock, the fog peeling upward in unraveling strands that revealed pastel porches, humming golf carts, sandy walkways, and the warm stirrings of island morning. The colors felt soft at first—muted pinks, worn blues, sun-washed whites—the haze had lifted, letting the day brighten around them.

Caleb opened the gate, his hand steady on the chains. "Safe travels now. Keep an eye on that weather—she'll change her mind quick on ya."

"Hey—anywhere you'd recommend for dinner?" Jesse asked as he stepped back toward the truck.

"Dajio," Caleb replied. "My aunt and uncle own it. Freshest seafood on the island. And that's where us locals'll be tonight."

"Locals and seafood? We'll be there," Sadie said, brushing a loose strand of hair from her cheek.

Boone muttered something into his hoodie, his gaze lingering on Caleb a moment longer.

As Caleb stepped away, Sadie watched him—not drawn to him, but to the ease he carried. The way people here seemed anchored to their place in the world. She felt a tug of longing, quiet but clear. Maybe that was part of why she'd come. Maybe the island held something she needed.

She climbed into the truck but didn't close the door yet. Let the salt air sit with her a moment longer.

Four years at Appalachian State. Ecology and Environmental Biology. She'd built her whole future around those peaks—grad school, Forest Service, a life in the high country. It had felt so certain.

Then last summer happened. The Duke Marine Lab internship. The researchers there studied coastal wetlands the way she studied cold-water streams. Something had cracked open in her that she hadn't been able to close.

A pelican glided low across the water. She tracked it until it disappeared.

She'd been looking at marine science programs. Coastal ecology positions. Places that felt nothing like home but called to her anyway. She hadn't told Jesse—hadn't wanted to add weight to whatever he was already carrying. But standing here, she let herself feel the question she'd been circling for months:

Not where do I belong?

But where could I belong if I let myself try?

The truck rolled forward into the village. Sunlight warmed the edges of cottages and oak branches, glinting off windows and sandy pathways. The sight tugged at Jesse—a filtered glow reminding him of dawn hitting pine needles back home. Different world, same quiet reminder: he stood on the edge of something new.

The truck rolled slowly through the village's main stretch. Gift shops crowded both sides of the narrow road—airbrushed t-shirts in windows, hand-painted signs advertising bike rentals and ghost tours, an ice cream shop with a line of sun-flushed tourists. Ocracoke Coffee Co. had its doors propped open, the smell of roasted beans drifting into the street. Everything felt carefully curated for visitors, bright and welcoming.

Jesse felt the performance of it—the island wearing a mask for tourists.

But as they turned onto a side street, the island's other face revealed itself. Live oaks arched overhead, their branches twisted and gnarled, draped with Spanish moss that swayed in the breeze. Cedar trees clustered near older cottages—weathered structures with screened porches where fishing nets hung drying, crab pots stacked like cairns, and faded buoys dangled from railings. A fig tree sprawled against one house, its broad leaves catching morning light. Yaupon bushes lined sandy yards, their small leaves dark green against sun-bleached wood.

An old man sat in a rocking chair on one of these porches, coffee mug in hand, watching them pass with mild curiosity.

A golf cart puttered by, driven by a woman in a floppy hat with a golden retriever riding shotgun, tongue lolling in the breeze. The dog barked once at Scout, who responded with an interested whine.

"I love it already," Sadie said, leaning forward.

The air smelled different here—less diesel, more salt and sun-warmed wood and something green from the cedars and oaks. Somewhere nearby, someone was cooking breakfast. Laughter carried from a porch. A child squealed.

The mountains held history, roots, expectation. This place held possibility.

"Tourist trap," Boone muttered, though the edge of his voice softened just slightly as he tried to clean the remaining gull mess from his hoodie.

"Maybe so. But it's our tourist trap today," Jesse replied, drifting into a smile.

Boone tapped his fingers on his knee, irritation flickering into something quieter before he hid it again.

Scout stuck her head out the window, letting the wind ruffle her ears as the rising sun painted the village gold.

The truck disappeared into the waking island.

Scout lifted her nose to the wind one last time, ears flattening against her skull. A small whine escaped her throat. She smelled something on that breeze. Something coming.

Chapter Two

Ocracoke Village

Late morning light filtered through the swaying limbs of live oaks and cedars, their branches stretching crooked and ancient across the Ocracoke campground. Sunlight broke into restless ribbons as the wind rustled the leaves, scattering gold and shadow across the sandy ground like shifting pieces of a mosaic. The air warmed quickly, salt rising from the Sound and mingling with the sweetness of marsh grass and the earthy scent of roots buried deep beneath the sand. The island was waking, stretching, pushing heat into the day. Somewhere unseen, a heron croaked from the marsh, its call tangled with the low hum of far-off boat engines.

Cicadas buzzed like distant static, threading through the stillness and settling into the background. The day felt as though it had already stretched into its full stride—a warm exhale settling over the campground, heavy with the taste of salt and sun-baked pine needles.

The truck sat tucked beneath a veil of shade, tailgate open, gear spread out with the purposeful disarray of people who'd done this many times before. Sleeping bags, dry bags, food totes, coils of rope, tent poles, spare clothes—the deliberate chaos of a trip balanced between adventure and survival. A faint breeze lifted the edges of tarps and nylon, making the gear seem to breathe in and out alongside the trees.

Jesse worked steadily, organizing equipment with quiet competence. He moved with the muscle memory of someone who had pitched tents and set up camp more times than he could count. Each stake landed with a sure, measured strike. Each strap was tightened, checked, then checked again, the tug confirming his certainty. His focus anchored him, as familiar as a trailhead back home, the sound of metal against damp ground pulsing steady at his core.

Sadie moved around him with light precision—quick steps, fast hands, sunlight catching in her hair each time she leaned or turned, rogue strands shining gold. She paused now and then to scan the campground: tents and RVs like colorful shells scattered in the sand, families arranging coolers, kids darting between the trunks of live oaks grown in shapes only the wind could explain. Every shiver of wind lifted the tent fabric, making it ripple like a living thing in the quiet grove.

Scout wandered the perimeter, nose close to the ground, tail swaying in rhythm marking the calm. She inspected shells, the grass, a stranger's forgotten flip-flop, then circled back toward the truck to ensure her people remained where she'd left them. Her loyalty walked the bounds of the campsite, paws leaving faint impressions in the sand that the wind would soon erase.

Their gear had changed over time. Jesse's tent: lightweight, expensive. Sadie's pack: new, technical. Boone's tent: same one from high school, duct-taped seams. His sleeping bag, one of Jesse's hand-me-downs.

Not that Jesse made him feel bad about it. Jesse just quietly paid—camping fees, food, gas. Always "splitting" costs that only one of them actually paid.

Sadie paused, looking up at the live oak overhead. Branches twisted in impossible shapes, bent by centuries of wind yet still growing. Spanish moss swayed though there was barely a breeze.

The tree had been here when the first settlers arrived. Was still watching.

Jesse felt it too—that sense of being observed. Not threatening. Just... noticed.

Sadie paused and looked down the narrow road that led toward the village. The island's rhythm was already finding its daily stride: golf carts humming past in clusters, tires whispering over sand; families biking with towels flapping behind them; joggers slipping in and out of yaupon-lined paths that swayed like green tunnels. The distant chime of a bell from a nearby bike echoed briefly, vanishing into the hush beneath the trees.

"We should get a golf cart. Be easier than hauling this truck all over."

Her voice carried a hint of mischief and possibility, as if she could already picture them laughing as they cruised through town, hair tousled from salt wind, sunlight flashing off the cart's roof, nothing important waiting on the other side of the day.

Boone crouched near the gear pile, sorting rope and gear. His movements were sharp, tension visible in the tightness at the corners of his mouth. He yanked at a knot harder than needed, the rope biting into his palms, shoulders rigid with effort.

"Why? We got wheels already."

Sadie shrugged as she tightened a strap on a dry bag, the nylon creaking softly in her hands. "It's the way folks get around here. Easier to park, fun, and we can go anywhere without worrying about the truck."

Boone snorted, rope fibers rasping between his fingers. "Yeah, well, they're probably fifty bucks an hour or something. Waste of money."

The words came out rougher than he intended, but he didn't correct himself. It was easier to let irritation pose as reason than admit the truth about what he couldn't afford.

Jesse drove a tent stake into the sand with a practiced, even rhythm—the thunk of metal into damp ground steadying everything it touched. "Boone, go get us a golf cart. We'll be done here by the time you get back."

Boone straightened, squinting over the truck bed. "You're serious?"

Sadie smiled at him, eyes bright. "Yeah. You'll love it."

Jesse slid folded bills into Boone's hand. The cash felt heavier than it should have. Pride flickered in Boone's eyes, followed by embarrassment as he pocketed the money. He hated needing it. Hated that Jesse always seemed to have more steady footing.

"Fine. But if they try to rob us blind, I'm walking back."

He tried to sound joking. It landed closer to a warning.

He headed down the sandy trail, boots kicking up fine dust that sparkled in the sunlight. Scout watched until he disappeared into the brightness, ears tilted forward as if waiting for him to turn back.

Jesse scratched her ears, fingers sinking into warm fur. "He'll be alright."

Sadie watched the road for a few quiet breaths before returning to the gear. The island tugged at her in a gentle, persistent way—like it had things to show her whenever she decided to look closer.

A faded shack sat crooked on the corner of a sandy lot, its paint peeling in long curls like old paper forgotten in the sun. Surf stickers and weather-beaten decals plastered the counter windows—board logos, island sayings, a hand-lettered sign reading, No shoes? No shirt? No problem... but bring cash.

Hand-painted price boards leaned against the railing. A rusted metal chair sagged beside the door, its webbing dried and cracked. The porch groaned under Boone's weight as he stepped onto it.

Rows of golf carts—turquoise, lime green, pastel pink, bright coral—gleamed under the sun. Some had coolers strapped to the back, some already dusted from morning rides, but all carried that easy island freedom Boone felt just beyond reach. The rubber tires pressed pale tracks into the sand, the scent of sun-warmed vinyl drifting up from the row.

Inside, a small box fan rattled in the corner, pushing warm air in circles. The smell of sunscreen, old coffee, and sun-toasted plastic mingled in the cramped space.

Boone placed his hands on the counter. "How much for a cart?"

The clerk—skin leathered by sun, ball cap bleached almost white—didn't rush. He completed a line on a rental form before lifting his eyes.

"Eighty for the day. Plus tax."

Boone recoiled, shoulders stiffening. "Eighty bucks? You serious?"

"That's the rate."

"You got anything cheaper?"

"Just bikes."

Boone huffed. "That's robbery."

The clerk didn't blink. "Some call it business."

Silence tightened. Boone opened his wallet, stared into the thin truth—a couple of crumpled bills, loose change. The rest was Jesse's, folded neatly in his pocket, heavier than money should be.

He snapped the wallet shut. "Forget it."

He turned sharply. The porch boards complained under his boots as he walked out into the glaring sunlight. His breath tightened, his throat dry. The taste of salt and dust stuck to his tongue, bitter.

I can't go back and tell them I didn't have enough money. I just can't.

The thought hit harder in the echo chamber of his mind.

If I go back empty-handed, they'll see right through me... same as always.

He shoved his hands into his pockets and kept walking, the sandy path crunching beneath his steps.

The side street curved away from the main road, half-hidden beneath the shade of bent cedars and scrubby oaks whose branches leaned inward like old friends sharing secrets. The pavement gave way to hard-packed sand and shell fragments that crunched softly underfoot. A turquoise golf cart sat parked in front of a weathered cottage, keys dangling from the ignition, a forgotten beach towel draped across the backseat.

No one in sight.

The breeze shifted.

His footsteps slowed.

He looked left. Then right. Quiet wrapped around him like a decision forming in the dark.

The turquoise cart sat there. Keys in the ignition.

Just borrow it. Return it tonight.

His throat tightened. Going back empty-handed meant watching Jesse fix it. Again. Meant Sadie's gentle understanding. Again.

Just for today.

He slid into the seat. Turned the key.

The motor hummed.

Borrowing. Just borrowing. I'll bring it back tonight. Before anyone knows.

Back at camp, the tents stood firm, guide lines pulled tight, shadow spilling cool and triangular across the sand. Scout rolled in a patch of softer dirt, paws kicking, nose dusted gray. Each joyful twist released little puffs of sand drifting through the warming air.

The faint whine of an electric motor approached—soft tires over shell and sand, a bright, cheerful sound weaving through cicada buzz.

***

Boone glided into the clearing with a grin that looked nearly effortless.

"Yeaaa... you got one!"

Sadie's voice burst out first, delighted.

Jesse nodded, approving. "Pretty work, Boone."

Boone stood a little straighter, shoulders loosening.

He hopped out with practiced casualness, tossing the keys in the air and catching them. "Bout time to take a lil ride and see what this island's all about."

Scout trotted over to inspect the cart, circling the tires, sniffing the rear platform. Satisfied, she hopped onto the front floorboard and sat, tongue lolling.

Sadie slid into the passenger seat, laughter bright under her breath. Jesse climbed into the back beside the cooler and daypacks.

The cart rolled forward down the sandy path, pine scent and Sound breeze trailing behind like a ribbon of invisible comfort.

The campground fell away—tents shrinking behind the framing arms of live oaks until all that remained was the hum of the motor.

The village unfolded in a patchwork of color and texture.

Narrow roads curved between salt-scrubbed houses with tin roofs flashing in the sun. Fig trees pressed close to picket fences. Merkel bushes bent in the steady southwest breeze. Oaks and cedars leaned in odd angles, shaped by storms until they learned to grow with the wind.

Other golf carts zipped past, passengers laughing, maps flapping. Kids waved from backseats, ice cream smeared across their cheeks. A man pedaled by on a beach cruiser with a fishing rod strapped to the frame and a tackle bucket swinging with each turn.

They passed a white church with a lean steeple and open windows letting the breeze wash through. A historic graveyard rested beside it, white crosses and aging stones baked in the sun, fenced by weathered boards leaning in surrender. Names long faded still held their ground against time and storms.

As they neared Silver Lake, the smell of the village shifted—suntan lotion and laundry gave way to heavier salt notes. The scent of diesel from charter boats mixed with fried seafood and hushpuppies from waterfront restaurants. Somewhere, a halyard clanged softly against a sailboat mast.

Sadie turned in her seat, taking in the windows filled with art, porches lined with potted plants, bikes leaned sideways against rails. A yard filled with fig trees cast patterned shadows across scattered lawn chairs and crab pots. A small boutique displayed hand-painted signs, each letter weathered from seasons of storms. Even the shadows on the road seemed different here—softer, slower.

They passed a porch where three old men sat in rockers, weathered faces turned toward the street. One raised a hand—slow, deliberate.

"Mornin'," the man called, his voice carrying that particular lilt Jesse had heard in Caleb. Not quite Southern. Something older. The words shaped different, like listening to history speak.

"Morning," Jesse called back.

Another voice drifted from an open window—a woman's down east brogue, thick and ancient. Jesse couldn't make out the words, but the rhythm pulled at something in him.

"Three hundred years," Sadie said softly. "The same English their ancestors spoke."

"The island kept it," Jesse said. "Wouldn't let it die."

Boone just drove.

The cart rolled past a small cemetery tucked between cottages—weathered stones leaning, names worn soft by salt and wind. A woman tended flowers at one grave, movements slow and reverent.

Sadie felt something shift in her chest. These weren't just dead people. These were the ones who'd stayed. Who'd chosen this sand and salt and storms. Who'd raised children here, died here. Generation after generation saying: This place is worth it.

"1847," she read from one stone. "She was younger than us."

"She probably never left the island in her entire life," Jesse said quietly.

The fig trees shouldn't grow this close to salt spray—wrong conditions, wrong soil. But here they thrived. Live oaks twisted by centuries of wind, each tree a record of every storm that tried to break it. Life refusing to die.

This wasn't the ordered succession of mountain forests. This was adaptation. Survival. Life bending itself to fit impossible conditions.

Sadie had spent four years studying mountain ecosystems. But watching these trees, these graves, these people who'd committed to this place for three hundred years—she wondered if resilience meant staying where you were planted, or learning to grow in new soil.

The island seemed to pulse with something. Not sound. Not sight. Something felt.

Jesse felt it too. The voices, the graves, the ancient trees.

The cart rolled on.

Early September. Nor'easter season.

***

The cart slowed as they passed a narrow lane leading toward the water. Fiddler crabs darted across patches of sand, disappearing into holes like living punctuation marks. A porch swing creaked lazily in the breeze. Laundry on a clothesline snapped like soft applause.

Sadie let the wind pull her hair back. For the first time in a long time, she wasn't thinking about the future—only the moment unfolding around her.

Jesse watched the village, then Sadie, feeling something inside him ease. The slow drift of a cart down a coastal street felt strangely familiar. The shade-and-sun pattern across the road flickered rhythmically over his knees, and he let that simple movement quiet everything that usually clattered inside him.

Boone drove with one hand on the wheel, the other resting on his knee, pretending a level of easy confidence he didn't quite feel. Passing other carts bolstered him—to them, he wasn't the guy who struggled to keep up. He was just another visitor moving with island rhythm. With each wave from a passing tourist, the tension in his shoulders eased.

They rolled under the shade of a massive live oak whose branches draped over the corner like a sheltering arm. Beneath it rested a small row of headstones, inscriptions worn soft by decades of wind and salt.

Further ahead, they passed the community square where artists set up small stands—driftwood carvings, shell jewelry, watercolor prints of the lighthouse. Scout perked up as the scent of funnel cake drifted from a nearby vendor. Children chased each other between picnic tables, their laughter rising like startled birds.

The cart coasted toward the harbor, the water shimmering through gaps between houses. Charter boats rocked at their slips. Masts pointed like thin white spears toward a sky that seemed impossibly wide.

Boone slowed the cart, letting the view widen as if offering it to the others. Even he couldn't deny the effect of the place, how the harbor somehow felt both familiar and unreachable, like a dream slipping into the shape of something real.

***

The lighthouse rose above the treeline like a white sentinel—curved white brick shimmering in the afternoon sun. The narrow path that led to it was quiet, flanked by marsh and scrubby growth.

Boone eased the cart into a sandy pull-off. Sadie and Jesse stepped out, the crunch of shells beneath their feet. Scout trotted ahead, tail wagging as she sniffed the mingled scents of marsh mud, grass, and open water.

Up close, the lighthouse felt even older. Hairline cracks in the whitewash, tiny windows set high in the tower, the thick base shaped by centuries of wind—all spoke of storms survived.

Sadie tilted her head back. "Feels like it's been here forever."

"Two hundred years, give or take," Jesse said.

She traced a fingertip across the plaque listing dates and keepers' names. She imagined men climbing narrow stairs in candlelight, watching storms slam against the Sound, deciding when to stay and when to pray. The weight of it pressed into her—commitment to place, to duty, to something larger than oneself.

Jesse stood at the base, palm flat against sun-warmed brick. Two hundred years. The stone held heat like memory.

For a moment—just a flicker—he could almost feel them. The men who'd climbed these stairs every night. The ones who'd kept the light burning when nor'easters roared in from the Atlantic.

Generation after generation. Keepers' names on that brass plaque—men who'd committed their lives to this tower, this light, this dangerous strip of sand.

What would that feel like? To know exactly where you belonged?

The teaching job had a deadline. Next Friday. Accept or decline.

September. The month when nor'easters began. When summer ended. When decisions locked in.

Portsmouth waited across that water—the ghost village, the thin veil, the place that had pulled at him before. But Caleb's warning echoed: King Tides this week, storm building, don't cross in bad weather.

The lighthouse didn't answer. Just stood there, white and permanent.

"Here," Jesse said, lifting his phone. "Get in front of it."

Sadie backed up, laughing softly as Scout sat beside her at the last moment. Jesse snapped the picture. "Tourist mode activated."

Boone stepped into frame long enough for a picture of all three. The lighthouse towered behind them, Scout posed at their feet. For a moment, they stood aligned—three friends framed against white stone and open sky.

An osprey cried overhead, circling wide, then drifting toward Silver Lake.

Then the moment released them, and they climbed back into the cart.

The shell road carried them away, wind slipping through their hair as the hum of distant boat engines pulsed through the afternoon.

****

On a seemingly forgotten part of the island, the road narrowed. The island quieted.

Sadie shifted uneasily, eyes tracking the narrowing road ahead. "Why does it feel like the trees got quiet?"

No one answered.

The clearing appeared without warning. Silence pooled beneath the branches. Jesse felt his skin prickle, a cold knot settling under his ribs.

Dolls. Everywhere.

Strung from low limbs by twine. Propped on fence posts. Tied to porch rails. Sun-faded. Salt-stiff. Plastic skin cracked like dried riverbeds. Some missing limbs. Some missing eyes. Some with hair so tangled it resembled seaweed left too long in the surf.

They turned slowly in the breeze, as if they'd been waiting for an audience, faces shifting with the faintest movement of air.

Glass wind chimes clinked softly above the porch, the sound brittle and sharp. Plastic limbs tapped wood with thin, eerie clicks. A rocking chair moved in slow, creaking rhythm across warped boards.

Unprovoked.

Boone stopped the cart.

Sadie stepped out, unease unfurling across her features. Scout followed, tail tucked low, ears pinned flat, a low vibration rising from her chest—more felt than heard.

Jesse and Boone stayed seated longer than necessary. Crossing the line from cart to clearing felt like stepping into a story older than themselves, the kind told in whispers after dark.

A pale woman sat in the rocking chair, half-hidden in shadow. Her silver hair trailed in thin strands, drifting like worn sea foam, the ends catching the last of the afternoon light. Deep lines carved her face—the kind etched by squinting into storms, not laughter.

When she spoke, her voice crackled. "The island is watching…"

Her hand lifted toward a cluster of dolls.

Sadie followed her gaze.

Three dolls: two male, one female. Their faded clothes fluttered. Their painted faces turned with the shifting wind—arranged in a grouping that felt too familiar, almost reflexively recognizable.

"Are these… yours?" Sadie asked, voice small.

The woman raised a trembling finger. No words. Just pointing.

Jesse's throat tightened. The resemblance wasn't literal—but it didn't have to be. The grouping alone drew a cold line through him.

Silence weighed heavy.

A breath of wind shifted the dolls. One turned just enough for light to catch its cracked face, the painted lips split in a permanent, uncertain half-smile.

Scout whimpered, pressing against Sadie's leg.

Boone's heartbeat thudded in his teeth, heavy and insistent.

Jesse felt the uncanny certainty that the island wasn't merely welcoming them.

It was studying them.

"Too weird for me. Let's get out of here."

Boone's voice broke the spell.

Sadie scrambled into the cart, Scout leaping in beside her. Jesse lingered for a heartbeat longer, transfixed by the way the dolls twisted on their strings—like warnings shaped into human form.

Then he tore himself away and climbed in.

Boone hit the pedal.

The cart shot ahead, tires spinning through sand, shells crunching beneath the weight. The dolls jerked violently in their wake.

The trees closed around the road behind them like a curtain falling.

The farther they drove, the easier it became to breathe. Village noise—distant laughter, a horn, a gull's cry—drifted faintly back, threading through the open windows.

But the unease stayed.

Boone's hands tightened on the wheel. The stolen wheel. The three dolls—two male, one female—hung in his mind.

"That was messed up," he muttered.

"It just felt... wrong. Like we weren't supposed to be there." Sadie responded.

"Coincidence." Jesse said firmly. "Old woman making stories fit. That's all."

But his voice carried an edge.

Boone said nothing. The cart hummed beneath them—borrowed, stolen, temporary. Like everything else about this trip.

As the road widened again and the afternoon sun broke through the canopy, the three of them sat in a weighted quiet. The air felt warmer but not comforting, like a held breath finally released. Boone kept his eyes fixed ahead, jaw clenched. Jesse lifted a hand to rub the back of his neck, where the hairs still stood upright. Sadie wrapped her arms around herself, trying to shake the lingering image of the dolls' twisted faces.

The cart hummed on.

The island resumed its noise.

But the hush they carried from that clearing followed them still.

Scout, shifting restlessly on the floorboard, pressed her nose to Sadie's knee, her breath warm against salt-stained denim. Sadie smoothed her fur with absent fingers, gaze fixed on the road ahead, her jaw set with a tension she didn't speak.

Only when the cart turned onto a sun-bleached street lined with fig trees and the sharp tang of brine filled their lungs did some of that weight begin to lift. Jesse drew in a deep breath, the salt air working into his chest, loosening what the clearing had left behind. For a moment, he closed his eyes against the sun, letting the warmth press the unease back into the corners of his mind.

The island's sounds crept in again—the slap of flag halyards, the drone of a distant outboard, the murmur of conversation from a porch. Life resumed its shape.

Chapter Three

Night in the Village

Warm, humid air wrapped around Ocracoke like a soft blanket as night settled over the island—the kind of heat that didn't press hard but lingered, as if the island quietly said, Stay awhile. The sky melted into a soft violet haze before full darkness arrived, the world brushed with lavender and bruised blue, giving porch lights and lamp-lit windows a warmer glow.

Lantern-style lights flickered across the gravel outside Dajio, their warm halos suspended in the mist-laced air like fireflies caught between breaths. Humidity softened the edges of everything—the glow, the shadows, the sound of footsteps crossing the patio—making the place feel dreamlike and close. Gravel crunched underfoot, each step muted beneath the weight of moisture in the air, and the scents of salt, fried hushpuppies, and summer jasmine drifted together in invisible threads.

Inside, guitar music drifted through the open doorway—low, rhythmic, threaded with laughter, clinking glasses, and the unhurried beat of coastal life. Conversations rose and fell like gentle tides, slipping against the background sounds of silverware, footsteps, and the soft bustle of the kitchen.

Boone eased the golf cart into a parking space, the gravel crunching beneath the tires as Jesse and Sadie climbed out. Scout padded down beside them, tail swaying, nose lifting toward the rich scents drifting from inside—grilled seafood, butter sizzling on cast iron, herbs crushed beneath busy hands. The smells rolled out into the night like warm invitations, promising comfort after a day that had already begun to tug at their edges.

As they approached the entrance, the wooden steps creaked under their feet. The lights overhead cast gentle halos across the porch railings, illuminating flecks of sand clinging to their shoes. Scout sniffed the air again, tail rising with approval, her eyes bright in the porchlight.

Sadie stopped on the steps and turned to face them both. "Okay. Tonight we're not thinking about tomorrow. No plans, no worries, no decisions. Just this." She spread her arms toward the glowing porch. "Deal?"

Jesse smiled. "Deal."

Boone grunted, which she chose to interpret as agreement.

Caleb stepped into the doorway as if he'd been expecting them. Sleeves rolled to his elbows, posture relaxed, his grin matched the easy rhythm of tidewater finding its path. His silhouette was haloed by the glow from inside, the lines of his face sharpened by golden light.

"You found it."

Sadie smiled, voice soft but bright. "We couldn't miss it. We smelled the seafood cooking before we ever saw it."

Caleb's gaze lingered on her a heartbeat too long—not bold, not claiming, just quietly observant. Jesse noticed. Boone noticed harder, shoulders shifting forward with a tension he tried to hide.

"Your dog's welcome out on the deck," Caleb said. "We keep water bowls out there."

Boone's response snapped like a twig under tension. "We're here to eat, not talk."

Caleb didn't flinch. "Try the shrimp and grits. Best on the island."

Sadie brightened instantly. "Then that's what I'm having."

A hostess waved them through. Caleb stepped aside with a small, knowing nod.

"Hang out after," he said, voice light but certain. "The Dune Dogs play tonight. Good music—should be fun."

His sincerity held no angle.

String lights glowed above the patio, reflections quivering across glasses of beer, sweet tea, and melting ice. The dusk air blended with the soft lights to create an intimate glow. Distant guitars and laughter mingled with the croak of tree frogs, weaving a living tapestry against the dark.

Scout curled beneath Sadie's feet, her body relaxed against the wooden planks. She exhaled a deep, contented sigh, ears flicking toward the guitar drifting from the porch. The cooling boards radiated the day's last warmth beneath her belly.

Sadie looked around, breathing in deeply, her eyes shining in the lamplight. "This place feels... easy."

Jesse followed her gaze, the lights flickering overhead catching in her hair and the condensation trailing down glasses around them, droplets pooling on scarred wood. "That's the island talking."

Boone, though, scanned the crowd with rigid intensity, shoulders tight, jaw set. His eyes bounced between strangers' faces, but always returned to the doorway.

"You notice he's always around?" he muttered.

Sadie frowned. "Who?"

"Your new friend, Caleb."

Jesse lifted his hand, weary. "Boone, not tonight, bro."

Their plates arrived—shrimp and grits steaming in fragrant spirals, butter melting into soft curls, spices blooming warm into the night. The smell softened the air around most tables.

But not theirs.

Caleb appeared again with an easy walk, posture relaxed, voice warm. "Everything good?"

Sadie lit up, genuine joy glowing in her expression. "Perfect! So glad we came here."

Her tone warmed in a way Jesse hadn't heard all day. Caleb noticed.

He nodded toward Boone's plate. "Came all this way for a burger? How was it?"

Boone stiffened.

A visible shift—jaw tightening, fingers curling against the table edge.

"Fine. Do you think you own this place, or do you just like hovering around flirting with other men's women?"

The patio fell quiet. Conversations halted. Even the music beneath the lights seemed to dip a note lower.

"Boone," Jesse hissed, disbelief edged into his voice.

Caleb's expression thinned to something calm, respect still intact despite the insult. "I told y'all my aunt and uncle own this place. I'm just makin' sure you're taken care of. That a problem?"

Boone met his gaze—brittle, hollow, angry.

"Not unless you make it one."

A tense beat stretched between them.

Caleb stepped back carefully, palms open. "Y'all enjoy your night."

Sadie's appetite faded. Her shoulders sank. Her fork hovered, untouched.

Warm porch lights cast soft halos across the planks. The band tuning up on the screened porch played gentle notes that drifted on the breeze—warm guitars, mellow harmonies, a rhythm that settled into the bones. The smell of night-blooming flowers edged in, mingling with the salty tang of marsh water and the distant smoke of a cookfire.

Caleb approached Sadie with measured strides—respectful, not intruding. "Supper turn out alright?"

Sadie nodded. "It was amazing."

He handed her a folded slip of paper—not sly, not flirty, but purposeful. "My number. Call if you need me."

Sadie blinked. "Need you?"

Caleb glanced toward the harbor, the joking tone replaced by something older, steadier. "Wind's shifting northeast in a couple days. Storm's building offshore—a real Nor'easter." His voice dropped. "Tomorrow should be fine for crossing. Calm. Beautiful, even. But don't linger on Portsmouth. When that wind shifts, it shifts fast. I've seen what those storms do to folks caught on the water."

It wasn't an invitation. It was a local reading the signs the way his grandfather had, and his grandfather before him.

Sadie felt something tighten in her chest—gratitude and the sudden sensation of being looked after.

Jesse stepped onto the porch behind her. "Dinner was fabulous. Good to see ya again, Caleb."

"You too, Jesse."

Sadie tucked the paper into her pocket. It felt heavier than it should have.

Something about this island made her feel seen, and she didn't know whether she wanted Jesse or Boone to notice that.

The Dune Dogs finished tuning, their final plucked chord drifting into the warm air like a lantern lifting skyward. The first notes of their opening song rippled across the porch, smooth and mellow, shaped by years of salt air and long summer nights. The melody hummed beneath the wooden planks, settling behind their ribs like something alive.

Sadie felt the music instantly—not as noise, but as recognition. The rhythm loosened something inside her, smoothing out the edges of the day. Her shoulders dropped, her breath eased. She found herself leaning forward, elbows lightly touching the railing, eyes glowing beneath the warm porch lights.

Jesse settled beside her, his posture softening for the first time since they'd reached the island. He didn't move much—Jesse was never the dancing type—but he absorbed the music, his foot tapping softly in the shadows.

He watched Sadie sway to the music, her face open in a way he rarely saw anymore. Something in his chest tightened. Not here. Not yet. Maybe not ever, if Portsmouth didn't give him the clarity he'd come looking for.

He'd known it since they were twelve. That summer on the French Broad when they'd flipped the canoe and she'd come up laughing, river water streaming down her face, and something in his chest had shifted permanently.

But knowing and saying were different things.

Saying meant risking everything—the friendship, the ease, the way they moved through the world together. Saying meant watching her decide if he was worth loving back. And what if the answer was no?

What if Portsmouth was supposed to tell him something? What if the island—this place that pulled at him in ways the mountains never had—was supposed to make things clear? Where he belonged. Whether he could tell her.

He watched her sway to the music, Caleb a few feet away, and felt time running out.

September. The teaching job. The storm coming.

Everything was about to change, and he still hadn't said the one thing that mattered.

Caleb stood a few feet away, respectful of their space but clearly absorbed in the moment. He tapped his boot heel to the beat, nodding along, a faint grin tugging at the corner of his mouth. Now and then he glanced toward Sadie—not in a way that crossed lines, but in that natural, easy acknowledgment shared by two people enjoying the same unexpected spark in the air.

Boone stood stiff.

His crossed arms pressed hard against his chest. His jaw was tight. Each strummed chord scraped at something raw inside him that he couldn't explain, couldn't control. Every time Sadie smiled—every time she angled closer to Jesse or Caleb—Boone's pulse ticked louder in his ears.

The song closed with a flourish. Applause rose warmly around them—light, easy, full of small-town appreciation. Boone didn't clap.

The second song kicked up faster—a foot-stomping reel that sent couples spinning across the porch. Sadie grabbed Jesse's wrist before he could protest.

"No. You're dancing."

"Sadie, I don't—"

"You do tonight."

She pulled him into the crowd, and for three minutes, Jesse forgot about Portsmouth, forgot about Friday, forgot about everything except Sadie's hand in his and the way she laughed when he stepped on her foot.

When the song ended, they were both breathing hard, grinning like idiots.

"See?" she said. "You can have fun."

"I never said I couldn't."

"You didn't have to."

Caleb watched from the railing, a quiet smile on his face. Boone watched too—arms crossed, jaw tight, not clapping.

The third song began slow—a deep, longing melody with notes that spilled into the night like a tide rolling under starlight. The singer's voice dipped warm and low, threading through the air with the feel of stories lived and retold.

Sadie closed her eyes, letting the music imprint itself on her. Jesse watched her quietly, admiring how freely she took in the world. Caleb watched the band but couldn't help the occasional sideways flicker of attention.

Boone watched all of them.

He no longer heard the music. He heard only his own pulse.

When the applause faded, Boone exhaled sharply—the only release he allowed himself.

"Aren't y'all ready to go? We have a big day tomorrow."

And just like that, the spell shattered.

Sadie's smile dimmed. Jesse straightened. Caleb stepped back.

The warm patio lights glowed behind them, a retreat receding into shadow as they moved away.

Sadie stopped first. The parking space sat empty, the gravel undisturbed except for the ghost of tire tracks leading away. For a moment, no one spoke. The absence of the cart felt louder than any sound.

The cart was gone.

"Where's the cart?" Jesse asked.

"Boone, didn't we park it here?" Sadie said.

"Course we did."

"Maybe someone moved it?"

Boone folded his arms. "Or maybe the owner came and took it back."

Sadie froze. "What do you mean, 'the owner'?"

Jesse stepped forward carefully. "Boone... where exactly did you get that cart?"

Silence stretched between them.

Boone exhaled sharply. "Doesn't matter now."

But it did.

"It matters if it was stolen—Boone, seriously!" Sadie burst out. "What are we gonna do now? Walk?"

"That's exactly what we're gonna do," Boone shouted.

Sadie shook her head, anger coloring her voice. "Gosh, Boone. I can't believe you."

Jesse stepped between them, voice calm. "Let's just let it go. Big day tomorrow."

They started walking.

Howard Street stretched before them like a corridor carved through time, a narrow ribbon of pale sand winding beneath the low, twisting arms of ancient live oaks. The night deepened around them quickly, swallowing the last traces of yellow porch light along the narrow lane. In the absence of artificial glow, the island seemed to grow older. Their footsteps softened into the sand, dulled and muted, as if swallowed by generations that had walked this same path.

The dirt lane was uneven and rutted, its edges pressed in by slanted white picket fences that leaned inward like tired guardians. Some slats were cracked or missing entirely, leaving dark gaps where thick shadows pooled. Others tilted forward as if bowing toward the road, their peeling paint revealing old layers beneath. Every so often, small family grave plots emerged within the enclosures, tombstones huddled together as though drawing close for warmth, their carved lettering flickering in and out of visibility under the shifting light.

A faint moonbeam cut through the density of the oak canopy above, catching threads of Spanish moss that swayed lazily overhead. The moss looked almost alive in the dimness, curling and drifting. The overhanging limbs created an archway that felt both sacred and unsettling.

Sadie slowed her steps, instinctively drawing nearer to Jesse. She could feel the history pressing in on her—not as a threat, but as an awareness that countless stories lay buried beneath the sand. Some part of her felt watched, not by anything sinister but by time itself. The closer she looked at the crooked fences and the weather-worn graves, the more she felt she was walking through a place that remembered every voice that had once whispered here.

Scout moved ahead cautiously, paws brushing through sand and dried leaves. Her tail dipped low. She sniffed along the ground, pausing at each fence line, ears flicking at sounds too soft for human perception. Now and then she let out a quiet rumble, not a warning—more like unease curling through her muscles.

Jesse felt a tingling along the back of his neck. He'd walked through forests at night, hiked stretches of mountain paths in the deep dark, but this felt different. The darkness wasn't empty—it was inhabited, dense with the echo of generations. The sandy road held footprints of the living and the dead, and the tombstones marked their final resting place.

Boone walked farther behind, dragging his footsteps, shoulders tight, the weight of his earlier choices pressing on him as tangibly as the humid air. The silence around him felt accusatory. He kept his eyes fixed on the path ahead, but the shadows at the edges tugged at him, whispering reminders of things he couldn't admit out loud.

A soft murmur drifted toward them from deeper down the lane. Voices. Slow, deliberate, echoing against the old wood and moss. The three of them paused instinctively. Scout's ears pricked forward, her body stiffening with attention rather than fear.

Then, the faint glow of lanterns appeared around a bend—a warm procession of moving light weaving through the low branches. Moments later, a ghost tour emerged into view, the guide at the front carrying a lantern that cast long, trembling shadows across his audience. The group walked in a loose cluster, their shoes crunching softly in the sand, their faces illuminated in the warm, shifting glow.

As they passed, the guide's voice rose, clear enough to drift toward Jesse and the others like a story carried on wind. "...and it's said that some nights on Howard Street, the old Ocracoke families walk with you. Folks have claimed to see figures moving between these fences, pale as moonlight, watching from the corners of their eyes. They say the dead don't haunt out of malice here—just memory."

A few people in the group drew closer together. Someone whispered a nervous laugh. Another held up a phone for a picture but lowered it again, perhaps realizing the camera could never capture the strange, reverent atmosphere of the place.

The guide continued, his lantern swinging slightly with each step. "Many believe the spirits along this street never left because they lived their whole lives right here. They built their homes here. Buried their kin here. Survived storms here. They belonged to this sand, to these trees, long before we came along."

The words drifted over them, settling into the branches above, the moss responding with the barest, breathlike sway.

Sadie's skin prickled. Not from fear, but from the sensation of stepping momentarily into someone else's tale. She watched their lanterns gliding by, and listened to their voices and soft murmurs.

As they hesitated, the guide's words clung to them.

Jesse felt it first—that same sensation from the lighthouse. The keepers who'd climbed the stairs every night. The families who'd chosen this sand, these storms, generation after generation. Not just living here. Belonging here.

He pressed his hand briefly against one of the weathered fence posts at the edge of a graveyard. The wood was warm, like it still held the memory of hands that had built it.

Sadie stood with her arms folded, breath slow. She could feel them—the ones who'd stayed. Who'd buried their children in this sand, rebuilt after hurricanes, refused to leave. Three hundred years of commitment.

As the ghost tour's lanterns receded down the lane, their glow caught a lone gravestone—set apart from the others, leaning slightly as if tired from standing so long. Sadie felt drawn to it, as if she were meant to see it. The name was worn but legible in that fading light: Jesse Dixon. 1872--1899. Died in the line of duty. U.S. Life-Saving Service.

She stopped. Read it again.

Jesse Dixon.

"Hey," she said quietly, touching Jesse's arm. "Was anyone from your family from here?"

Jesse shrugged, eyes still on the path ahead. "My dad spoke of having ancestors from down here, but he would never say for sure. Why?"

Sadie glanced back at the stone, but the lanterns had rounded a bend now, leaving it in shadow.

"No reason," she said. "Just curious."

But she didn't forget the name on the gravestone. How could she? There was no name that was ever more familiar to her.

Scout moved cautiously, nose working. She felt the depth here, the layers of scent humans couldn't name. Old earth. Old wood. Old stories pressed into sand.

Boone kept his distance, gaze lowered. Even the dead seemed to be watching him tonight. Judging. Knowing.

The stolen cart. The lies. The shame that followed him.

He walked faster, trying to outpace what he couldn't admit.

The quiet grew thicker, pressing gently at their backs. Each crunch of sand beneath their feet sounded amplified. Every creak of a fence post or rustle of moss seemed magnified beneath the low lull of cicadas. The night played tricks with distance—the path ahead appearing to narrow and widen with each dozen steps.

Sadie walked with her arms still folded lightly across her chest, mind swirling with images she couldn't quite shake. Jesse stayed close, posture firm but eyes scanning. Boone kept his distance, gaze lowered, every so often glancing sidelong at the shadows.

The canopy began to thin at last, and the warm glow of lanterns appeared ahead—soft amber light flickering from scattered campsites. The tension from Howard Street loosened in their shoulders as they stepped out of the old darkness and into a gentler night. Voices carried faintly through the humid air, mingled with the distant hush of the ocean and the smell of charcoal drifting between the trees.

Scout trotted ahead with renewed confidence, tail lifting as if sensing they had crossed some unseen threshold. The walk from the village had worn all of them down, and the simple glow of lanterns felt like mercy.

They reached their tents, the fabric dimly reflecting the nearby campsite lights. No one spoke. The silence wasn't heavy—just the natural settling that follows a day stretched too far. Sadie slipped off her shoes and let her toes sink into the cool sand. Jesse dropped his pack and exhaled slowly. Boone stood a few steps away, staring into the shadows.

The island felt different here—still watchful, still old, but quieter.

Scout circled once and settled.

One by one, they disappeared into their tents.

Tomorrow they would cross to Portsmouth. Tomorrow, Jesse would stand where the veil was thin and see if the island had anything to tell him.

The ghost tour guide's words still moved through him: They belonged to this sand, to these trees.

Scout sighed and settled deeper into the sand.

Somewhere beyond the dunes, the Sound lapped quiet and steady against the shore—calm for now.

Chapter Four

The Crossing

Jesse stood at the water's edge, bare feet sinking into wet sand, staring across the Sound toward Portsmouth Island. Morning sunlight washed over Ocracoke Beach in warm golden sheets, catching the distant dunes in soft focus. Gulls circled overhead, their calls sharp and bright in the early air. The Sound breathed in soft rhythm, waves folding into the shore with the steadiness of a heartbeat—a rhythm Jesse always felt deep inside himself, as though some part of him had been tuned to this place long before he ever set foot on the island.

Portsmouth pulled at him. Steady. Ancient. Certain.

The johnboat and canoe rested side by side at the tide line, hulls still damp from morning dew, ropes neatly coiled, paddles laid out with care. Beyond them, Portsmouth hovered across the water, its dunes blurred into soft silhouettes by distance and morning haze. Even from here, its presence felt old.

Behind him, Boone snapped a strap tight across a dry bag in the john boat. "Scout can ride with me to even out the weight." He patted the bow. "Come on, Scout. More room up here anyway."

Scout bounded over without hesitation, paws splashing through the shallows, tail wagging. She leapt into the aluminum boat with practiced balance and planted herself at the bow, ears forward, body steady. Boone rested a hand on her back—a gesture small enough to overlook but grounding enough to matter. She let out a soft huff, leaning into his palm.

Sadie planted her hands on her hips, studying the far shore with quiet intensity. A breeze lifted a few strands of her hair, turning them into thin golden threads against the morning light. The scent of warm sand and drying salt drifted around her. "Hard to believe we're actually doing this."

Jesse inhaled deeply, letting the smell of the Sound settle into him. "Been a long time coming."

He could almost see their younger selves in the shimmer of morning light—barefoot kids racing down muddy riverbanks, imagining adventures they believed they'd always be brave enough to take.

Some truths didn't need words.

"Let's see if you guys can keep up with me."

He tried the familiar smirk, but it didn't land. Something restless pressed at the edges of him—not fear, but an agitation he couldn't name. Boone didn't handle stillness well; silence made room for thoughts he tried hard to outrun. Tension curled through his chest, an unwelcome pressure beneath the calm sky. He tugged another strap, as if a stronger pull might steady whatever moved in him. The metallic ring of the buckle carried too far in the quiet.

Sadie rolled her eyes lightly. "Let's take our time, Boone. No hurry."

He didn't answer. His silence spoke more honestly than any reply. Sadie noticed the way his jaw shifted. She didn't push. Not yet.

Together, they stepped forward to push the boats into the water. Warm sand gave way to cool softness beneath, and the first chill of Sound water curled around their ankles—sharp enough to jolt every nerve awake. Jesse welcomed the bite. Sunlight danced along the waterline, bright flashes scattering with each shift of their feet.

Jesse steadied the canoe while Sadie stepped in, bringing the paddle to rest lightly across her knees. Her breath caught for a heartbeat—anticipation, excitement, something in between. The canoe felt as delicate as a thought, yet sturdy enough to carry them. When she turned back toward Jesse, an unspoken question passed between them: Ready? He nodded once and climbed into the stern. The canoe took his weight like a welcome.

Their supplies were lashed down with knots Jesse's father had taught him—knots tied on riverbanks, knots tied during storms, knots tied with hands smaller than his now. A faint memory flickered behind the work: his father's voice guiding, correcting, teaching. The loops and hitches held more than gear.

With a final push, both vessels slid free of the sand and into the Sound. The water accepted them without fuss, drawing them smoothly into its slow rhythm. Their hulls glided outward, leaving ripples that stretched wide before dissolving into glass again. A faint hum of wind pushed against Jesse's ears, carrying the scent of open water and faint hints of unseen marshland in the distance.

Sunlight scattered across the surface like bright coins.

The first strokes carried them past the shallows where sand patterns glimmered below. Tiny crabs lifted puffs of sediment as they scurried away from the shadows of the boats. As the water deepened, the glassy clarity shifted into cool greens and calm blues, revealing long columns of light reaching downward in shimmering shafts. The Sound felt alive—a shifting, breathing world beneath them.

He leaned forward slightly, voice softened by memory.

"You can see every shell down there."

"Water this clear always makes me feel like a kid again."

Sadie dipped her paddle, sending silver ripples fanning out across the Sound. "Feels like we're floating on glass."

Their strokes found an easy rhythm—Jesse's steady power guiding the canoe, Sadie matching his cadence without effort. The rhythm took focus—not conversation. Arms pulled, shoulders burned with the good ache of work remembered from mountain rivers. They'd paddled miles of the French Broad this way, wordless and synchronized, saving breath for the effort. This crossing would be no different.

Boone rowed harder than needed, each pull straining through the aluminum frame. Sweat gathered at his hairline despite the cool lift of air off the water. His breath came harder now, each stroke pulling deep. Three miles with no motor meant earning every yard. He kept his eyes on the island, using the distance to outpace thoughts he didn't want to face. Motion quieted the noise inside him. Stopping invited it back.

He forced a grin across the water. "Don't get all sentimental on me—you'll slow your paddle."

A tightness flickered across Boone's eyes before he looked away.

Scout stood tall on the bow, testing each shift in wind. She was the only one not working. Jesse and Sadie's paddles dipped and pulled in steady rhythm, their breathing matched to the strokes—efficient, trained, no energy wasted on words. Seabirds cried overhead, their voices carrying across open water like distant calls from another world. Every new scent pulled Scout's attention. A line of pelicans skimmed the surface far off to the east, their wingtips grazing the water in perfect formation.

They crossed into deeper water where turquoise gave way to dark cobalt. Here, the paddles sounded different—muted, absorbed by depth.

Scout's ears shot forward.

She barked once—sharp, insistent—her body rigid at the bow. Boone's hand went to her back, steadying. "What is it, girl?"

Before anyone could answer, the water exploded.

A dolphin surfaced ten feet from the canoe, its back arcing smooth and dark through the light. Then another. And another. Four—no, five—their bodies rolling through the water with effortless grace, dorsal fins slicing the surface in perfect rhythm.

"Holy—" Boone's voice caught.

"Dolphins!" Sadie's paddle froze mid-stroke, water streaming from the blade.

They surfaced again, closer now, their sleek bodies turning just beneath the hulls. Jesse could see them—gray shapes gliding under the canoe like shadows made solid, their forms distorted by refraction but unmistakably there. One rolled onto its side, dark eye visible for a heartbeat, looking directly up at him.

A high-pitched squeak cut through the air—then another, a cascade of clicks and whistles that sounded almost like conversation. The dolphins were talking. Not to each other—to them.

Scout barked again, leaning so far over the bow that Boone spoke up. "Easy girl!"

But she wasn't scared. Her tail whipped side to side, whole body wiggling with excitement. She barked again—three quick yips—and one of the dolphins answered with a chirping trill.

"She's talking to them," Sadie breathed.

"They're talking back," Jesse said, wonder threading through his voice.

The dolphins swam in exaggerated loops beneath both boats now, their patterns intricate and purposeful. They dove under the john boat, surfaced between the vessels, circled the canoe in a figure-eight that felt almost choreographed. Water sprayed from their blowholes—sharp bursts of mist and sound.

One broke the surface inches from Scout, eye to eye. Scout went still, nose extended, sniffing the salt air. The dolphin clicked softly—a quieter sound, intimate—and Scout whined low in her throat, the sound of a dog trying to speak a language just beyond her reach.

"I can't believe they're getting this close," Boone said, his usual bravado stripped away, replaced by raw amazement. "This is crazy."

"It's like they're welcoming us." Sadie's voice was hushed, reverent.

Jesse felt it too—something more than animal curiosity. The dolphins moved with intention, their attention focused, specific.

A larger dolphin—the matriarch, Jesse thought—surfaced directly ahead, body parallel to their course. She held there for three breaths, dorsal fin steady as a compass needle pointed toward the island.

Jesse felt something lock into place—not understanding, but certainty. Whatever waited on Portsmouth, he was meant to find it.

Then she dove, her tail lifting clear of the water in a graceful arc before sliding beneath.

The others followed, one by one, their bodies disappearing into the deep blue.

The last lingering clicks faded. The water smoothed. Scout whined once more, staring at the empty space where they'd been.

"Did that just happen?" Sadie's laugh was breathless, disbelieving.

Boone shook his head slowly, a genuine smile breaking across his face. "That was..."

"Unreal," Jesse finished, his paddle dipping into water that felt different now—blessed, somehow. Alive in a way that went beyond biology.

A quiet settled over them, a reverence Jesse felt in the bones of the canoe. He dipped his hand briefly into the Sound, feeling the temperature change—colder.

Calm water wasn't always safe water. His father's voice drifted back like a caution carried on the wind: Always know the difference.

The Sound widened around them, an expanse of open space that felt bigger than maps suggested. The shoreline behind them shrank into a thin line, the houses of Ocracoke turning into tiny shapes tucked behind dunes. The air thickened with that peculiar stillness that comes with mid-Sound crossings.

Sadie glanced back, noticing the subtle crease between his brows. She didn't ask about it. Instead, she offered a small, steadying smile.

Portsmouth Island sharpened as they drew nearer. The low dunes and cedars at the entrance—simple, wind-bent, unassuming—rose in soft contours, their faces brushed smooth by years of shifting gusts. Sea oats trembled on the ridges, bending to a breeze that hadn't yet reached the boats. Farther down, beyond these first modest dunes, the larger dune stood in distant profile, a muted giant watching quietly from afar.

Boone rowed with restless force, watching Jesse and Sadie glide in harmony. Something inside him tightened at the sight—old insecurities, old shadows he thought he'd buried. He rowed harder, as if outpacing an echo. His oars pulled heavy arcs through the water, the Sound resisting just enough to make him feel the weight.

The water brightened again as they entered the shallows. The current stiffened, asking for strength. Jesse and Sadie dug deeper, their bodies shifting into the familiar rhythm carved by a childhood of river trips. Their paddles brushed the sandy bottom now and then, sending up soft clouds of pale sediment.

A warm breeze carried the scent of hot sand and sun-scorched driftwood as the island drew near. The first dunes loomed closer—not towering, but present, shaped by wind and memory.

Their hulls slid across the pale bottom.

THUMP.

The canoe kissed the sand. Boone's john boat grounded moments later with a heavier thud.

Boone stepped into the shallows, feet sinking in warm, shifting sand. He dragged the john boat higher with a grunt. Sunlight cut sharp angles across his face, revealing something raw beneath his posture.

Sadie stepped out next, the water swirling around her ankles. Portsmouth stretched before her—vast, quiet, untouched. The small dunes ahead rippled with shadows, their tops etched by the restless hands of the wind. Grasses whispered against one another in low, trembling voices.

As Jesse's bare feet sank into Portsmouth's sand, a quiet thrum ran up through his legs—the same grounded, unmistakable feeling he'd carried since childhood riverbanks. It felt less like arriving somewhere new and more like returning to a place that had been waiting for him.

Scout froze mid-step, ears pitched forward, staring at something beyond the dune line that none of them could see. The air changed—not wind exactly, but a shift in pressure, like the moment before a door opens in an empty house. Jesse felt it move through him, a recognition that went deeper than memory. The island knew he'd returned. And for just a breath, the knowing went both ways.

"I don't care what happens the rest of the day," Sadie said softly. "That was worth the whole trip."

Jesse joined her, eyes scanning a shoreline that mirrored a memory so perfectly it jolted him. The light struck the dunes in the same golden angle he'd seen years ago. Even the smell—that blend of hot shell, and warm salt air—matched what lived in his mind. "Feels the same... just like last time."

He'd been seventeen. His father had brought him here on a camping trip, just the two of them, a week before Jesse left for college. They'd stood on this exact beach at dawn, and his father had said something Jesse hadn't understood then: "Places like this show you who you are, if you're brave enough to look." Jesse had nodded, thinking he understood. But he hadn't. Not until years later, when he realized he'd been running from clarity his whole life—too afraid to name what he felt, too careful to risk what mattered. Portsmouth had waited. And now, standing here again with Sadie beside him, he understood why his father had brought him. Some truths needed witnesses. Some required islands.

Boone drove his oars upright in the sand. "Hell of a finish."

Sadie smiled, letting the last of her tension fall away. "We made it."

Jesse looked toward the low dune line muted only by the occasional Merkel bush, sunlight pouring across their tops like liquid gold. The larger dune farther down the beach rose faintly in the heat shimmer, a quiet sentinel waiting for its role later. "This is it."

The words left his mouth heavier than expected.

Scout bounded ahead, her pawprints dotting untouched sand until the wind began erasing them. Sadie knelt beside her, fingers finding the soft place behind her ears.

"I forgot places could feel this untouched."

"We really did it. All those river trips as kids got us ready for this moment. You're a boat dog now, Scout. Time to explore."

They hauled both boats above the tide line, feet sinking into the warming sand. The wind whispered across the low dunes, carrying the low pulse of the ocean beyond—a distant heartbeat beneath the island. Jesse felt the faint rumble of surf vibrating up through the sand beneath his feet, a physical hum that carried through the ground like memory.

Backpacks settled onto shoulders. Water bottles shifted.

Jesse pointed toward the glowing dune line ahead—the smaller dunes tugged them forward with gentle promise. "Let's explore the beach first. It's such a beautiful day."

"Let's do it," Boone said, something in him loosening—not entirely, but enough.

With Scout leading, leaving prints the wind would soon erase, they hiked toward the ocean. The sand warmed under their steps, soft ridges rising and falling beneath their feet, every footprint briefly holding the memory of their passing before smoothing away. Sea oats clattered softly in the sea breeze as they passed, dry stalks whispering together. The nearer ocean grew louder, its steady roar swelling over the low dunes, threading salt into the air.

Farther down the beach, the larger dune towered in the distance, its silhouette hazy with heat, rising above the shimmering line where sky met sand.

Somewhere out beyond the breakers, a subtle shift in wind carried the faint smell of a storm gathering offshore—a quiet whisper of what waited beyond the horizon.

The island noticed.

Even if they didn't yet.

Chapter Five

Portsmouth Island

S cout stood alert beside Jesse on Portsmouth's shore, nose lifted to catch scents carried off the dunes. Midday sunlight poured over the shoreline like molten glass, turning every grain of sand into a pale shimmer. Heat rippled upward in soft, wavering curtains, bending the horizon and making the air feel thicker than normal, almost alive.

Portsmouth Island had a way of pressing on a person, not with weight but with presence—quiet, ancient, unbending. Jesse felt it in his bones. On this day, even the wind seemed to move slower here, as though it had traveled a long distance and was finally allowed to rest. On the mainland, air moved fast and busy; here, it drifted, as if it had all the time in the world to decide where to go next.

Sound carried differently, too. Every crash of surf, every distant gull, every whisper of grass felt magnified by the sheer emptiness of the place, as if the island were a great, shallow bowl collecting and holding everything that dared to make a noise.

The boats lay drawn well above the tideline, both faded and scarred from years of hard use. Behind them rose the foredunes—soft, wind-tilled ridges of bleached sand dotted with sparse sea oats and Merkel bush trembling gently in the light breeze. Every stalk bowed and lifted again, as if nodding in slow agreement with some rhythm only the island understood. In every direction stretched solitude: a thin, shimmering margin where sky met water, and sand met time. There were no houses, no piers, no boardwalks—just the raw edge of a barrier island standing between ocean and Sound, doing the job it had done for centuries without ever asking for thanks.

Something in Scout's posture said the island had a flavor unlike anything she'd ever known—salt and sun and something older, something she instinctively respected. Her ears flicked with every distant gull cry, every faint rustle in the grass. She inhaled deeply, chest expanding as she sorted through layers of smell: dry dune sand, faint fish from the tideline, warm marsh breath drifting over from the Sound side, and that hard-to-name wildness that lived in places untouched by pavement. Her tail gave a slow, thoughtful wag—the measured acknowledgment of something that mattered.

Sadie shaded her eyes, sweeping an arm slowly along the open shoreline. The gesture was wide and sure, like she was presenting not just a beach, but an entire world laid bare just for them. "Let's explore the beach and go climb that giant dune to get our bearings," she said. "Following the beach around to the left should take us right down to it."

Jesse nodded, already feeling the pull of the landscape. The dune she pointed toward rose in the distance like a pale, sun-struck shoulder against the sky, a landmark as commanding as any mountain ridge back home. "Yeah. Let's do it."

Boone snorted—too sharp, too quick, out of proportion to the stillness around them. "I'm all for checking out the beach, but are we here to climb dunes or find the lost village?"

Sadie didn't even look at him. Her gaze held to the shoreline and the distant dune, as if giving Boone any more attention would hand him a power she wasn't willing to concede. "Lead the way, Jesse."

Jesse saw the small movement, almost lost beneath the brightness of the morning—the quick clench, the muscle jumping at the hinge of Boone's jaw. The island seemed to notice the tension and tuck it somewhere in its shifting sands. The breeze thinned for a heartbeat, carrying their silence down the beach like something fragile and unsettled.

They headed left along the vast ocean-facing shore, Scout trotting between them—her stride light, her tail bright with excitement, as if the island had opened a door just for her. She darted ahead a few paces, then doubled back, checking on each of them in turn as if she'd just been promoted to lead guide. The shifting sea breeze lifted her fur, and she released a quiet bark, more breath than sound. It blended into the rush of surf, a small, content exhale swallowed by the larger breathing of the island.

The ocean beach opened before them like an untouched frontier—wide, bright, and unbelievably vast. Nearly a hundred yards of white sand separated the rolling surf from the first rise of the dunes. That distance felt both inviting and humbling, a great empty canvas waiting to record their footprints. The dry sand near the dune line was the color of bleached bone, powdery and loose. Each step there loosened tiny avalanches that slid back into their own depressions, erasing the edges as soon as they made them. Locals called it sugar sand, and it lived up to the name—beautiful, delicate, and deceptively difficult to cross. It clung to ankles and slipped out from under heels, swallowing energy with each slow, sinking stride.

But closer to the water, the ground firmed, smooth and cool beneath their soles. Here, the sand held them without resistance, packed by years of tidal reach and retreat. When waves rolled in and thinned back out, they left a brief sheen that mirrored the sky before fading into a dull, pearly matte.

Here lay the treasure.

Shells—thousands of them—scattered in natural drifts, untouched by human hands. Whelks with curling pink interiors. Smooth olive shells catching the sun like polished stone. Fragile angel wings, whole and perfect. Scotch bonnets, rare elsewhere but abundant here, lying like small miracles in the tideline glitter. Each step risked crushing something that had taken years to form and only seconds to break. The sheer abundance bordered on overwhelming, like walking through a cathedral where the floor itself was stained glass.

Sadie knelt immediately. Her knees pressed into cool, damp sand, and she braced one hand to steady herself while the other hovered over the shells like she was afraid to disturb a sacred arrangement. "I've never seen anything like this," she breathed.

"Some people say this is the best shelling beach on the whole East Coast," Jesse said. He watched her fingers move carefully among the shells, the way her expression softened into open wonder. Seeing the beach through her eyes made the claim feel less like a brag and more like a simple truth.

Sadie lifted a perfect whelk and let out a quiet, reverent laugh. The shell filled her palm with unexpected weight, its spiral smooth where the ocean had polished it clean. "I believe them."

Boone kicked at a shell fragment, sending it tumbling toward the surf. The piece spun end over end, catching light before a small wave reached up and took it away. He didn't look at what he'd broken loose; he stared out past the breakers instead, his face set in a hard line that didn't match the beauty around them.

They walked on, the ocean's roar constant and powerful. The sound tunneled into them, filling their ears until it became less a noise and more a condition of existing here. Gulls wheeled overhead, cutting long arcs across the sky before dropping toward the ebbing waves. Their shadows flashed over the sand like quick, fleeting ghosts. Far beyond them, framed in the shimmering distance, rose the great dune.

The land rose in a long, gentle swell, climbing higher and higher until the dune towered over the beach like the rib of some ancient sleeping beast. Even from afar it felt monumental. It held a quiet authority, as if it had been present for every shipwreck, every storm, every crossing. The early English explorers had climbed dunes just like this, believing they were standing between two oceans—one to the south, one to the north—because the marsh and Sound were so vast they looked like open sea.

Now Jesse saw exactly what they saw. Standing at its base felt like facing a small mountain made entirely of time.

Sand gleamed under the high sun, sculpted into delicate ripples by centuries of wind. Each ridge and trough gave the impression of motion frozen mid-flow, as if the dune might start sliding again at any moment. One side of the dune fell away sharply—wind-cut, carved into a steep, dangerous face that dropped like a cliff. Time had bitten at it relentlessly, shaving away its side grain by grain. One wrong step near that edge could mean disaster. From where they stood, Jesse could see where the sand had sheared clean, exposing subtle layers within the dune like rings in a tree trunk.

The ascent would not be easy.

But it would be revealing.

Boone eyed it. A bead of sweat slid from his temple along his jawline, catching briefly in the stubble there before dropping into the collar of his shirt. "Doesn't look like much to me."

His tone carried too much edge, too much effort not to care.

Sadie smiled softly. "It's beautiful."

Jesse agreed. But he also felt something else—a quiet knowing, a recognition, as though the land remembered every footstep that had ever touched it. For a moment, he imagined the ghost impressions of all those who had come before them: sailors, keepers, lifesavers, fishermen, families. All of them climbing to this same ridge for the same reason—to see.

Climbing the dune was like climbing warm, shifting snow. Their feet sank deep, sliding backward with every attempt to gain ground. Fine sand spilled into their shoes, gathering under arches and grinding at their heels. The sun pressed hard against their backs. Even the mild wind couldn't cool them. It only moved the surface sand into tiny rivulets that ran downhill like liquid light, cutting faint, temporary paths around their footprints.

Jesse's calves screamed after the first twenty feet. Each step cost twice the effort it should have, his boots sinking deep before finding any purchase. Sweat trickled down his temples. He could hear Sadie's steady breathing behind him, rhythmic and determined, and it kept him moving.

Scout led the way, bounding effortlessly, never sinking the way humans did. She floated over the surface, weight distributed perfectly on four agile paws. She paused every few yards to check on them, ears perked, tail high. Her tongue hung out the side of her mouth, but her eyes were bright, energized by the challenge and the vantage point still waiting above.

Jesse pushed upward, his shirt stuck to his back, the dampness cooling only when a stray gust found its way beneath the fabric. Boone came last, muttering curses between clenched teeth, each one swallowed by the breeze before it could take shape. His breaths were louder, shorter, marked by frustration as much as exertion.

The sand burned through his socks where it had spilled in, each grain of friction a small punishment. He wanted to be first to the top—needed to be—but his body fought him with every step.

Near the top, the dune narrowed, the breeze breaking gently across its crest. It felt ancient... and alive. Fine grains clung to their shins and bare arms, lifted and thrown by the invisible hands of the wind. The steep drop on one side was close enough for Jesse to feel a small pull in his gut, a primal warning to stay back from the edge.

When they reached the top, the world opened in every direction.

Jesse bent forward, hands on his knees, pulling air into his lungs in deep, grateful gulps. Sadie stood beside him, chest rising and falling, a sheen of sweat on her forehead catching the sunlight. Even Scout panted heavily, tongue lolling, but her tail still wagged. The view made everything worth it.

His father had fished these waters. Had probably stood on this same ridge, squinting at the same horizon. Jesse wished he could tell him: You were right, Dad. This place shows you who you are.

But this view was enough. This moment. These people.

It was like stepping up into a new dimension, one where the island finally revealed its full shape.

To the southeast: the Atlantic, rolling in wild, relentless lines of white-tipped force. Patches of blue and green twisted together in restless knots, signs of shifting winds or deeper currents. The horizon looked less like a line and more like a boundary between two living things—the sea and the sky—pressing against each other in endless negotiation. Sadie's breath caught. "That is... wild. Look at the ocean. It looks so angry today."

"Doesn't look that angry to me," Boone grumbled, though his voice thinned around the edges. The scale of what lay below them slipped past his defenses, even if he refused to admit it.

"That's not a place I'd want to end up," Jesse said.

"Me neither," Sadie agreed. She hugged her arms briefly around her middle, not from cold but from an instinctive reaction to the raw power displayed below.

To the northwest: the marsh stretched endlessly—at least a mile of shimmering spartina grass, shifting green to gold in the late-summer sun. From up here, it looked deceptively solid, a quilt of life and stillness. Sunlight flashed in thin, secret channels cut between the stands of grass, glinting like broken mirror shards scattered by some giant hand.

To the northeast: Ocracoke—small, distant, but unmistakable. The shape of the village huddled low against the horizon, softened by distance and heat. The faint suggestion of the lighthouse pricked at Jesse's memory, all the stories he'd heard about the place turning slowly into something real.

To the southwest: the narrow ribbon of the island blending into Core Banks, a thin line holding ocean and Sound apart. It looked fragile from up here, like something that could be wiped away with one bad storm, and yet it had endured countless ones already.

Sadie sank to her knees. Sand slid around her shins as she settled, hands pressed into the crest of the dune as though she needed physical contact with it to believe what she was seeing. "Water break."

Jesse unslung his pack. The strap came away from his shoulder with a faint, sticky tug where sweat had gathered beneath it. Sadie opened hers. Scout trotted over immediately, licking her lips, her body language shifting from sentinel to hopeful beggar in a single heartbeat.

Jesse poured a stream of water into his palm and offered it. Scout drank eagerly, tail brushing against his ankle. Her tongue was warm and rough against his skin, her trust as simple and absolute as the sky above them. Sadie took long, grateful pulls from her bottle before tucking it neatly away. The water left a cool path down her throat, cutting through the dry heat that clung to her.

"Let's make sure we leave no trace up here," she said. "Whatever we pack in, we pack out."

"Always," Jesse said, sliding his empty bottle into the side pocket. The word carried a little more weight than the simple principle of Leave No Trace.

Boone drained his water in three aggressive gulps and let the bottle fall into the sand. It landed with a dull, wrong-sounding thud against the fragile crest.

Sadie froze. Jesse stared at him. Even the wind seemed to pause. For an instant, the ridge felt like a held breath.

"Boone," Jesse said quietly. "Pick it up."

For a moment Boone didn't move. His eyes flicked from the bottle to the marsh, to the ocean, anywhere but Jesse's face. Then, jaw clenched, he bent, snatched the bottle, and shoved it into his pack.

A small thing. But the island took note. Down in the marsh, a breeze skimmed an extra ripple through the grass.

Jesse pointed north. "There it is. The village."

Boone squinted. The sunlight made him lift a hand to shield his eyes as he followed Jesse's line of sight. "That's it? Has to be three or four miles away."

"Maybe not that far," Sadie said. Her voice carried the gentle contradiction of someone used to smoothing edges rather than sharpening them.

"We could hike the beach along the edge of the inlet. Easy walking."

"Longer, but easier," Jesse added. The idea of the firm sand at the water's edge, the known rhythm of waves beside them, settled into his chest like the safer choice.

His shoulders squared a fraction, his stance shifting subtly as if he were bracing for an argument he'd already decided to win. "Going straight there across the marsh is shorter. Much shorter."

"Shorter, but soft," Jesse said.

"And wet."

The push to prove he could take the harder, more direct route flared in him, a familiar instinct born far from this island but perfectly at home in its unforgiving spaces.

The breeze shifted.

The island held its breath.

They descended the dune in sliding steps, sand pouring around their ankles. Sometimes the ground gave way faster than they expected, forcing quick corrections, little half-stumbles that sent small cascades tumbling down the slope. The mood had changed. The air felt heavier. Even Scout sensed it—her tail low, her ears swiveling, uncertain. She stayed closer to Jesse and Sadie than before, glancing back over her shoulder toward Boone as if trying to keep them all within one protective circle.

At the bottom, the landscape stretched open again. As they faced the ocean, to the left lay the ocean beach they had followed earlier, broad and shining beneath the sun, its vastness somehow less comforting now that they knew how quickly a single choice could divide them. Behind them stood the tangled wall of Merkel bush—dense, twisted, unforgiving. Shadows pooled under their branches, dark and still, even in the heat of midday.

And that was when Boone made his choice.

Jesse saw it in his eyes first—that hard flicker of determination mixed with something darker. Boone's jaw set, his shoulders squared, and Jesse knew what was coming before he took the first step.

Boone veered sharply toward the Merkel bush, not slowing, not thinking—only moving. His boots chewed into the sand with a kind of finality, kicking up little puffs behind him.

"Boone, wait!" Jesse called. His voice carried down the open strand, thinned by distance and swallowed by the surf.

"Let's stick together!" Sadie said, voice rising. There was more in it than simple concern about logistics. Something about the sight of him turning away struck her deeper than she'd expected.

Boone didn't turn. "I'll get there faster. I'll be waiting on y'all."

Jesse took three quick steps forward. "Boone, seriously—the marsh is dangerous. We don't know how deep the mud is. We don't know—"

"I know how to take care of myself," Boone cut him off. His voice carried an edge that had nothing to do with the route and everything to do with the space that had opened between them over four years. "Been doing it my whole life. Y'all take the easy way. I'll take the short cut."

Sadie's voice softened, trying once more. "Boone, please. It's not about easy or hard. It's about—"

"I said I'm fine." Boone's tone dropped to something almost gentle, like a door closing quietly instead of slamming. "See you at the old village."

The Merkel bush swallowed him almost instantly, the thick green branches closing behind him like a gate. Leaves scraped his shoulders and arms, and then he was simply gone, hidden by the dense tangle.

Jesse stood frozen, staring at the space where Boone had disappeared. His chest felt tight, not from the climb but from something closer to dread.

Scout froze, looking between the two paths. Between Boone... and Jesse. Her paws shifted restlessly in the sand.

Sadie touched Jesse's arm gently. "I don't know about you... but this way feels right."

Scout chose Jesse and Sadie. She stepped to their side with a decisive little huff.

And the island did too. The breeze coming off the ocean felt a fraction cooler, a fraction kinder, circling Jesse and Sadie like an unseen escort.

***

Boone pushed into the Merkel bush with stubborn determination, branches clawing his arms and snagging his shirt. Each snag felt like the brush itself was trying to turn him back, but he gritted his teeth and muscled through. Shade gathered around him, but it offered no relief—only heat trapped between woven limbs. The still air there smelled of resin and leaf mold, a close, green heaviness that stuck to the back of his throat. Three times he followed false openings that ended in tangled dead ends. Each time, he had to backtrack, fighting the irritation rising inside him like a second kind of heat.

Then he saw it—a break in the brush, and beyond it a faint double rut in the earth. Waterlogged. Overgrown. Mosquitoes hung in the air above it like drifting smoke.

An old four-wheeler path.

He forced his way through and stepped into the marsh.

At first glance, it was beautiful—a mile of shimmering spartina grass, green with golden tips catching the light. The grass swayed in long, slow waves, as if the whole marsh were breathing under some deeper command.

The village floated beyond the far edge, the white steeple rising above the grass. From here, it looked close enough to touch, a crisp, bright promise against the haze.

Boone stepped forward.

The marsh stepped back.

His boot sank deep into suction mud. The ground held it with a slow, powerful grip, releasing only after he yanked hard. The sound it made—wet, reluctant—followed him with each step. Each new step took more energy than he wanted to admit. The earth here behaved like a living thing.

Mosquitoes descended in a cloud. They whined in his ears, dive-bombed his neck and wrists, found the tender skin just above his socks. He slapped at them angrily, but for every one he crushed, three more seemed to take its place. Humidity wrapped around him like a wet blanket, sealing in his frustration. Sunlight bounced off shallow ponds. The marsh stretched endlessly, broken only by small bodies of water he never saw until he was nearly in them.

Something caught his eye—a glint in the spartina ahead. Pale. Familiar.

A plastic bottle, half-buried in the mud. Not his. Couldn't be his. He was miles from the dune.

But it looked exactly like his.

Boone's stomach turned. He told himself it was the heat, the exhaustion, the way the marsh played tricks. He didn't look at it again.

He stumbled into a thigh-deep pool, panic flaring as the mud clawed at his boot. Warm, murky water surged up around his leg, and for a heartbeat his mind flashed a quick, unwanted image of being swallowed whole. He grabbed spartina, heaved himself free, breath rasping. Mud slurped as his boot came loose, trying to keep him. His lungs burned in protest at the sudden effort.

Halfway across, exhaustion set in—deep and punishing. His legs shook. Sweat dripped down his spine, salt stinging the raw places where the marsh had already scraped him. The village shimmered, no nearer than before. The dune behind him looked both far away and not far enough. Going back would mean admitting he'd made the wrong choice in front of people who already doubted him. Going forward meant fighting a place that didn't care one way or the other.

Beautiful, yes.

But merciless.

And Boone kept going, because turning back felt worse than pushing forward. Each dragging step became less about distance and more about pride—about proving to himself, to the island, to whatever else might be watching that he could carve a straight line through a world that refused to be convenient.

***

Meanwhile, Jesse and Sadie stepped back onto the ocean beach, the vast shoreline opening before them like a promise. The sound of the surf rose to meet them. Scout raced ahead, barking at gulls, splashing in the swash where waves curled over smooth sand. Her paws kicked up small fountains of water that sparkled briefly before falling back into the sea.

They headed northeast along the tideline. The shelling remained extraordinary—perfect whelks and bonnets gleaming in scattered pools. Some lay half-buried; others rested on the surface, gleaming in the sun. Sadie stopped to lift a golden-hued shell, letting sunlight slide across its surface. Its spiral seemed to hold an entire sunset inside it.

The emptiness of the beach struck her again.

No footprints but theirs.

No noise but the sea.

It felt like the world had paused just for them. Time thinned out, stretched between one footstep and the next. Jesse felt it, too—the odd sensation that the life they'd left behind on the mainland existed in a different dimension altogether, one that couldn't quite reach them here.

After a time, the beach began to curve. The ocean's roar softened. The angle of the shoreline shifted, and with it the character of the water. Waves rolled in with a slightly different cadence, less headlong, more restrained.

The inlet was coming.

***

The sand grew firmer, packed by tidal flow. Their footprints here were shallower, more defined, as if the island wanted to remember this part clearly. Shells thinned. The scatter became a sparse grammar of broken pieces, the intact treasures now mostly behind them.

The water turned green and gold. It reflected not just the sky, but the dunes behind them, gathering color from both worlds. On their left, low dunes and Merkel bush pressed closer. The vegetation leaned in toward the inlet as if drawn by the same quiet pull that drew Jesse and Sadie. On their right, the inlet shone in calm, rhythmic pulses. Small ripples chased each other toward the shore, meeting the sand with a soft, almost polite hiss.

Sadie breathed out slowly. The change in the air settled over her shoulders like a light shawl. "It feels different here."

"Yeah," Jesse said. "The inlet changes everything." His voice dropped a fraction, softened by the hush around them. He'd grown up hearing adults talk about inlets with a mixture of respect and suspicion, but standing here, he mostly felt awe.

A dolphin surfaced. Then another. Their sleek backs rose and dipped with unhurried grace. Water beaded and rolled off their skin in silver drops. Jesse recognized the markings on the matriarch's dorsal fin—the same pod that had escorted them across the Sound.

Sadie gasped. "Jesse—look."

Scout barked once, bright and excited. She danced in place, front paws hopping as if asking permission to chase what she knew she couldn't reach.

The dolphins paralleled their path as if escorting them up the inlet—close enough to see clearly, far enough to remain untouched. Every so often one would roll just enough for a fin to flash in the sun, a quiet, wordless acknowledgment of the strange little procession moving along the sand.

"It doesn't even feel like the same island from earlier," Sadie said.

"The dune felt wild. Powerful. But this? This feels gentle."

"Like the island is showing us both sides of itself," Jesse said.

Sadie smiled. "Maybe it is."

Two fishing skiffs drifted near distant shoals in the inlet, their silhouettes dark against the sunlit water. Men aboard them cast nets in slow, practiced motions. The nets opened like pale, translucent flowers before kissing the surface and sinking below. The scene felt timeless. It could have been today or fifty years ago; nothing in it needed a date to make sense.

Sadie looked at Jesse. "Not empty," she said softly.

"Just quiet."

They fell into step naturally. Close. So close their arms brushed, once, twice... then didn't drift apart anymore.

Scout circled them and nudged Jesse's hand, then Sadie's, tail wagging like she already understood what was happening. She seemed to be gently herding them together the way she might guide wayward sheep, except this task clearly pleased her more.

Sadie laughed quietly. "I think she approves of this walk."

"I think she approves of a lot of things," Jesse said. He let his eyes stay on Sadie a fraction longer than he might have back in the mountains, where the world was more crowded and it felt like someone was always watching.

Sadie looked at him—the slight tilt of her head, the softness at the corners of her eyes.

The island felt still around them, listening. Even the dolphins seemed to slow their pace, as if reluctant to move too far ahead of whatever was unfolding on shore.

Jesse's heart kicked against his ribs. How many times had he imagined this? A hundred river trips, a thousand shared moments, four years of distance that had done nothing to dull the want that lived in his chest like a steady ache. The island had given him clarity his whole life had refused to offer. Portsmouth was showing him what he'd always known but never had the courage to reach for.

His hand hung at his side, close to hers. Waiting. Hoping.

Then, without hesitation, Sadie reached for his hand.

Her fingers brushed his lightly. The contact sent a current up Jesse's arm. For a heartbeat, their hands hovered in that tentative space between maybe and yes.

The touch was tentative but sure, like testing the temperature of water she already knew she wanted to step into.

Jesse's hand opened. His fingers found hers.

They intertwined.

Sadie let out a breath she hadn't known she was holding. Her thumb brushed across his knuckles—once, twice—a small, unconscious motion that said more than words could. She'd been afraid to want this. Afraid to risk the friendship they'd built over years of rivers and mountains and shared silence. But Portsmouth had pulled the truth out of both of them, and now that it was here, in the warmth of his hand wrapped around hers, she couldn't imagine why she'd ever been afraid.

Scout let out a soft, approving bark, tail wagging so hard her whole back end wiggled. She danced around their legs in a happy circle.

Neither of them spoke. The moment didn't need words—it needed the sound of waves, the warmth of sun, the rhythm of their steps falling into sync. Jesse's thumb traced small circles on the back of her hand, and Sadie moved just slightly closer until their shoulders brushed with every step.

They walked hand in hand along the glowing inlet shore, dolphins pacing them, skiffs drifting in the distance, and the island welcoming them forward. The moment was small enough to miss from far away and large enough to change the shape of everything that came after.

***

Far to their left, beyond dunes, Merkel bush and cedar, across the shimmering expanse of the marsh, Boone fought another step.

And another.

And another.

The suction mud clung to his boots. It made a hollow, sucking sound each time he forced his foot free, as if the marsh were reluctant to give it back.

His breath rasped. Each inhale scraped his throat; each exhale left his chest feeling a little more hollowed out. Sweat mixed with the faint salt of dried Sound water on his skin, leaving a gritty film that the air refused to lift away.

Mosquitoes swarmed. They clouded in front of his face, speckled his arms, found every edge of fabric and skin. He swatted and cursed and pressed on, his frustration swelling to meet the unyielding drag of the marsh.

The village shimmered—close enough to see, too far to reach easily. Its white edges blurred and sharpened in the heat, like something half-real, half-mirage.

Jesse and Sadie walked toward connection.

Boone trudged toward consequence.

The island had split their paths, and none of them yet understood what that meant. But the land did. In the steady roll of the inlet, in the restless shifting of marsh grass, in the quiet, watchful dunes, Portsmouth

Island recorded every choice, every step, every small defiance—and waited patiently to reveal what it would all cost.

Chapter Six

The Life Saving Station

Sadie hiked ahead with Scout trotting faithfully beside her, the dog's posture alert but calm. Late afternoon light spilled across the tall grass. The sun clung lower on the horizon, turning dunes into broad, glowing shoulders rising and falling like the ribs of something ancient sleeping beneath the sand.

Jesse walked a few steps behind, watching her move through the landscape. The wind slipped through the sea oats in a hushed, steady breath, brushing the tops with a touch so soft it felt deliberate—as though the island inhaled and exhaled around them, an old rhythm pulsing beneath everything.

Even Scout seemed to sense the hush, her ears swiveling as she padded through the dune grass, nose catching the layered scents of salt, heat, and the faint musk of drying marsh. Every sound carried with a clarity that made the world feel both larger and more intimate: the whispering oats, the muted rustle of Sadie's pack, the shifting grains of sand beneath their steps.

The faint groan of an unseen shutter drifted across the abandoned village ruins in the distance, carried by the lingering breeze. Every dune, every sway of grass, every drifting fleck of sand felt aware of their presence.

The Portsmouth Island Life-Saving Station rose from the clearing like a structure suspended between centuries—salt-worn timbers, sun-baked shingles curled at the edges, windows clouded by storms long passed. It didn't look abandoned. It looked waiting.

They approached the porch, where a wooden placard leaned toward the path, its letters weather-softened but still resolute:

U.S. LIFE-SAVING SERVICE STATION — PORTSMOUTH ISLAND

Est. 1894 — Maintained by the National Park Service

The sign's edges were crusted with salt, the grain swollen from decades of coastal storms, each crack and warp telling its own story. Jesse brushed a thumb over the raised lettering as he passed, feeling the age of it—the quiet authority of a place built to face down the worst the ocean could bring.

Sadie slowed, something in the station's presence drawing her as though a hand had brushed her sleeve. Her eyes widened, reflecting the warm light that gathered on the roofline and traced every weathered edge. The building's silhouette cut against the sinking sun like a memory refusing to fade.

"It's beautiful. Like something from a dream."

Jesse studied the angles, the shadows, the way the structure seemed to lean slightly toward them, greeting them or judging them—he couldn't tell which. Every weathered surface whispered of storms survived, lives pulled from black water, men who had met impossible nights with grit and iron will. He felt small standing before it, humbled in a way he didn't fully understand.

"Or a ghost story."

Scout settled into a patch of sun near the porch steps, circling once before lowering herself onto the warm sand. She sniffed the boards cautiously, tail lowered but steady.

Jesse and Sadie climbed the porch, each board groaning under their weight—long, resonant creaks that echoed into the frame. The scent of salt and dry wood grew stronger as they stepped beneath the shadow of the roof.

Jesse placed his hand against the door. The wood felt cool beneath his palm, worn smooth by decades of hands pressing the same place. A subtle tingling moved across his skin.

The door groaned open, the sound rolling through the rafters like a release of breath held too long.

Dust floated in golden slants of fading sunlight, suspended like drifting stars. The air smelled of old canvas, dried salt, and timber that had stood firm through a hundred winters. Time didn't hang here—it gathered, thick as mist, settling into corners and beams, filling the room with reverent stillness.

Sadie stepped closer, her breath catching. Displays lined the walls—oilskins darkened by age, frayed lifebelts, wooden pulleys polished smooth by hands that once pulled them against roaring seas. Rusted tools rested in glass cases, their edges dulled but still holding the memory of use. Logbooks lay under soft light, their pages curled from humidity, ink faded but not forgotten.

Every object seemed to hum with the echo of storms long past.

"These men were heroes."

Her voice sounded small in the cavernous room.

Jesse nodded, eyes moving along racks of gear that once saved strangers through nights most people could never imagine. His chest tightened with something like reverence, or longing, or both.

"Whole crews trained just to rescue strangers in storms."

His voice softened, carrying a gravity shaped by the artifacts around them. For a moment he could almost hear phantom shouts—imagined oars biting into black water, boots pounding across wooden planks, lanterns swinging in howling winds.

They walked deeper into the station. The high ceiling arched above them, each beam scarred by time and work. An iron stove rested near stacked firewood, as though still prepared to warm crewmen after bone-chilling patrols. Rows of empty bunks lined one wall, blankets tucked tight—silent, pristine, waiting.

Near the far wall, oars leaned neatly at attention, their handles pale from countless grips—hands that once pulled against death and brought men home.

At the center of the room rested the life-saving boat—broad, heavy-built, its hull bearing scars shaped by storms long gone. It commanded the space like a slumbering giant. The boat's worn planks rose in slow, graceful curves, and Jesse felt a slow tug of awe pull at him from deep within.

Sadie stepped toward it, fingers hovering inches above its rim.

"They really went out in this?"

"In storms that would sink most boats."

Jesse's voice held awe, shaded with something deeper—something unspoken. He imagined men waist-deep in freezing surf, fighting to launch this boat into seas that wanted nothing more than to crush them. He felt pulled toward the gravity of what they endured.

Sepia photographs lined the wall—storm waves rising like black cliffs, boats nearly vertical, crews braced against furious wind and water, lanterns clutched in white-knuckled fists.

Sadie froze.

A crewman in one photograph stared out from the image. It was one of several on a wall with a placard hanging over them that read, "those who died in the line of duty." The fading light caught the image of his face.

He looked exactly like Jesse.

"Oh my gosh Jesse... that looks exactly like you."

Something pulled Jesse forward—an undeniable gravity. He stepped closer. His breath thinned. His reflection merged with the man's—two profiles aligning across two centuries.

A feeling moved through him, sharp and ancient.

A wild thought surged, unbidden and immediate: Was this a relative—or was it him?

A version of himself from another life? Another storm?

His hand reached toward the photograph without conscious thought, fingers trembling. The glass felt cold under his palm, and for a moment he could swear he felt the man inside reaching back—not with fear, but with recognition. As if some part of Jesse had always known this moment was waiting. As if Portsmouth had been calling him here not just to visit, but to remember.

The air in the station thickened. Time bent.

Then the vision hit.

Wind roaring.

Oars plunging into black water.

Lanterns swinging wildly.

Men shouting his name.

Spray stinging his eyes.

The boat lurching under him—alive with danger.

The cold bit through his jacket—no, through his oilskin coat, heavy with salt water. His hands were raw, bleeding where the oar had worn through skin. He could taste the storm: salt and fear and something metallic. Men's voices surrounded him, calling names he didn't recognize but somehow knew. The boat rose on a massive swell, tipping so far he could see straight down into black water—

A woman screamed from the wreck. He could see her pale hand reaching through splintered wood—

The hand. He'd seen that hand before—on the ferry, in a dream he'd dismissed as exhaustion. The same pale fingers. The same desperate reach.

It hadn't been a dream. It had been a memory. One that didn't belong to him.

His heart hammered against his ribs so hard it hurt. Real. This felt real.

Then Sadie's hand touched his shoulder, and the vision shattered like glass.

His arms tightened with phantom memory. The weight of the oars wasn't imagined; it felt remembered.

Lightning cracked across a dark horizon—and for a single impossible heartbeat, he was the man in the photograph.

His knees felt weak. Sweat had broken out across his forehead, cold despite the warmth of the room. His heart still raced with the phantom rhythm of rowing against death. For a moment he couldn't remember if he was Jesse Austin from the mountains, standing in a museum in 2024, or someone else entirely—someone who had stood on a deck in howling wind and pulled strangers from drowning.

The line between the two felt dangerously thin.

Jesse's fingertips trembled as they touched the glass.

"I've... seen him... he looks just like me."

Sadie moved closer, shoulder brushing his. Her voice softened with worry.

"Jesse... you're shaking."

"Yeah... Seeing that picture just hit me weird."

He swallowed, chest tight.

"Feels like he's looking straight through me... like he knows me... like it's me."

He forced himself to step back, but the air felt heavier now. Something subtle had shifted, as though the station itself had recognized him.

"You think any of your family were in the Life-Saving Service?" Sadie asked gently.

"Not that I know of. I barely know anything about my ancestors. But... anything's possible."

She let the thought hang there, suspended like dust in the golden light.

Sadie turned toward the ladder leading up to the cupola. Changing the subject with purpose.

"Wanna see the view from up there?"

The steadiness in her voice grounded him. She stepped onto the ladder, reaching for the first rung. Warm light washed over her as she climbed—slow, sure, graceful. The wooden rails accepted her hands as though countless others had gripped them through the decades, leaving them smooth and polished by time.

From below, Jesse felt something inside him tighten. The late light carved her silhouette into warm gold and soft shadow. Her hips shifted with each step, legs lengthening into lines shaped by movement and sun. Her shirt lifted slightly as she climbed, revealing a narrow line of sun-browned skin at the small of her back. Her calves flexed with each careful rise.

The simplicity of her movement felt breathtaking.

His mouth went dry. He'd known Sadie his whole life—known her as the girl who could out-paddle him on the French Broad, who laughed with her whole body, who saw things in the woods no one else noticed. But this was different. This wasn't childhood friendship or even the tentative hand-holding on the beach.

This was want.

Raw and undeniable and too big to pretend away.

The way the light caught her hair. The curve of her hip as she reached for the next rung. The casual grace of her movement.

Portsmouth was stripping away every careful lie he'd ever told himself about what she meant to him.

She wasn't his friend.

She was everything.

He drew a slow breath. God, she was beautiful.

Halfway up, she paused. She didn't turn immediately—she just felt him behind her. Then she glanced back, meeting his eyes.

"You coming?"

"Yeah. Right behind you."

His voice cracked just slightly.

The cupola opened around them like a tiny lantern room filled with gold. Windows wrapped the small space, gifting them a sweeping view of the island—dunes rolling toward the inlet, the Sound shimmering silver, Portsmouth's ghost-village soft in the distance.

It should have been breathtaking.

But Jesse barely saw the landscape.

Because none of it—not the water, not the dunes, not the wild sweep of the island—compared to the beauty standing inches from him.

Sadie turned toward him fully, her skin warm from the climb, her breath still uneven.

"You don't have to hide whatever that was," she murmured. "Not from me."

Jesse stepped closer without thinking, drawn into the small gravity she created.

Her hand brushed his arm—light, testing. His pulse jumped.

The cupola wrapped around them. Every breath she took seemed louder in the confined space. He could smell the salt on her skin, the faint cedar scent from her hair, something underneath that was just Sadie—familiar and intoxicating at once.

Her eyes searched his face, and he felt exposed in a way that had nothing to do with the windows surrounding them. She was seeing him. Really seeing him.

"I felt it too," she whispered. "Downstairs. When you saw the photograph."

Her fingers traced up his forearm, slow and deliberate. His skin ignited under her touch.

"I've been feeling things since we got here," he managed, voice rough. "Maybe before that. Maybe for years."

Her lips parted. Her breath quickened.

"Jesse..."

The way she said his name—

The tiny cupola made their closeness inescapable, tightening the air between them.

"Jesse..."

She said his name like she meant it—like she wanted something.

He leaned in, drawn toward her parted lips, the warmth radiating between them—

KA-THAM!

The slam of the station door downstairs cracked through the moment like lightning snapping a tree. Scout barked from below—sharp, frantic.

The moment shattered. Jesse's hands were still reaching for her, frozen in the air between them. His heart pounded so hard he could hear it. Sadie's face flushed, her chest rising and falling with quick breaths.

They stared at each other—desire and frustration and a question neither of them could answer.

Sadie jerked back, breath catching.

"I don't think we're alone here, Jesse."

They moved quickly.

Jesse led down the ladder, Sadie close behind. Their footsteps echoed through the hollow station, hearts still thudding. They swept the room with their eyes—corners, shadows, the hull of the boat—searching for any sign of movement.

Nothing stirred.

But something felt present.

Jesse glanced back at the photograph on the wall. The crewman's eyes hadn't moved—of course they hadn't. But for a moment, he could have sworn the man was watching them leave.

They pushed through the front door and stepped onto the porch in a rush. Sunlight hit them hard, grounding them.

They paused, scanning the clearing.

Movement rippled through the brush.

Sadie pointed. "Jesse... look. Boone made it."

Boone stumbled into the clearing like he'd crawled through the island itself. Every step from the marsh to here had been a fight—not just against mud and mosquitoes, but against a realization sinking deeper with each miserable yard.

The marsh hadn't just exhausted him. It had humbled him in a way that cut deeper than pride. He'd spent two hours trapped in a hell of his own choosing while they'd walked an easy beach, probably laughing together, probably not thinking about him at all.

Mud coated his legs. His clothes were wet with sweat and marsh water. His skin was welted with bites. He looked exhausted—defeated—war-torn.

He looked at Jesse and Sadie standing side by side on the porch, and something about their posture made his chest tighten. They looked... different. Like they fit together in a way he hadn't noticed before.

The island had split their paths for a few hours, and somehow everything had shifted.

He pushed the thought away.

Scout sniffed him warily, tail lowered.

Sadie rushed to him. "There he is..."

"You okay?"

"That marsh was hell. Mud, sinkholes... mosquitoes so thick I couldn't see. Felt like I was gettin' eaten alive."

"Looks like you did," Jesse said.

Sadie shook her head. "You should've come with us. The beach was perfect."

"I definitely made the wrong choice." His voice cracked with something deeper. "Seems like I'm always two steps behind y'all."

Jesse softened but didn't press.

"Come on. There's shade behind the station."

Sadie handed him a water bottle. He drank like resurfacing from deep water.

"You wanna see inside?"

"I'm worn out. Let's just get the campsite set up and chill."

"Alright," Jesse said.

Sadie planted her hands on her hips. "But guys, I really want to see the church and the village. So y'all suck it up."

"Alright, Sadie. Whatever you say."

Boone groaned. "Fine... I'm coming."

Sadie grinned. "Good. I didn't think y'all were gonna wimp out on me. Come on, Scout."

They followed the narrow path into deepening dusk.

The light thinned around them, trading the warm gold of afternoon for a softer, bluer tone that settled over the island like dusk. The world narrowed to a path of sand and trampled grass beneath their feet, to the faint crunch of sand and the whisper of stalks brushing their legs. Somewhere to their right, beyond the dunes, the unseen inlet breathed—a low, steady surge that rose and fell like a distant memory.

Jesse walked at the front edge of their small formation, with Sadie just a half-step to his right and Boone trailing a few paces behind. Scout ranged between them in loose arcs, her nose low, charting invisible paths through the shifting scents. From the outside, they might have looked like three friends settling into the quiet of evening. But inside Jesse's chest, the quiet had become anything but simple.

He could still feel the cupola in his skin—the heat, the breath between them, the moment just before. Now, walking beside her in the cooling dusk, he was hyperaware of every inch of space between them. Six inches. Maybe eight. Close enough that if he shifted his weight slightly, their arms would touch. Close enough to feel the warmth radiating from her skin. Far enough that the distance felt like torture.

His fingers flexed at his side, remembering the weight of her hand in his on the beach. Wanting more.

The door slam had broken the moment, but something inside him had already crossed a line. He had walked into the Life-Saving Station expecting history. He had walked out carrying something far more dangerous.

Sadie kept her gaze forward, but she could feel him beside her with every step. She could feel the heat of him beside her like a second sun. Every shift of his weight sent ripples through the air between them.

The space between their arms felt charged, a narrow corridor of heat and possibility. She replayed the cupola in flashes: the sway of low light across his face, the way his eyes softened when he looked at her, the breathless inch that had separated them right before everything fell apart.

And beneath those memories, another one flickered: their long walk down the beach earlier, their hands finding each other without effort or thought.

Scout brushed against her leg, grounding her with a simple, loyal presence. Sadie reached down to touch her, grateful for the uncomplicated steadiness.

Behind them, Boone dragged his feet slightly, the weight of the day pulling at him. His legs still stung from the marsh, his clothes damp, his pride bruised in ways even he didn't want to admit. But he wasn't so far gone that he didn't notice the strange hum in the quiet ahead of him.

He told himself he was imagining it.

But something felt different between them.

The way Jesse angled his body slightly toward Sadie when he walked. The way Sadie's hand swung a little too close to Jesse's, like she was testing something. The way they weren't looking at each other but seemed intensely aware of each other anyway.

It was the kind of awareness that came after something happened.

He couldn't say what.

But he felt it.

Sadie sensed Boone's eyes for a moment and subtly shifted a half-inch more space between herself and Jesse, a tiny adjustment almost invisible in the dimming light.

Jesse noticed her shift too. And it tightened something in him—not frustration, but longing tangled with fear. Boone meant something to him. Sadie did too. One wrong move, he knew, could fracture something important.

The path narrowed, pushing all three of them closer as the bushes thickened on either side. Fireflies blinked to life, scattered sparks drifting above the stalks like wandering stars. The island's breath cooled, evening settling with soft fingers across dunes and ruins.

Sadie's hand swung once, brushing Jesse's knuckles—so lightly she could have blamed it on the path. But it wasn't the path. They both knew it wasn't the path.

The contact sent electricity up his arm, made his breath catch. Her pinky finger hooked his for just a second—deliberate, testing, asking a question she couldn't voice aloud.

His finger curled back, answering.

Then she pulled away, and the loss felt physical.

His hand twitched, wanting to take hers, hold it the way he had on the beach. Wanting to feel that belonging again.

Instead, he curled his fingers inward.

They didn't speak.

They didn't look at each other.

But the space between them carried everything unsaid.

Jesse thought of the photograph—the man who looked like him, staring out from another storm. He thought of the vision, the way the oar had felt in his grip though he hadn't touched one. Everything about this island tugged at something deep inside him, pulling loose threads he didn't know he carried.

Sadie felt something similar. The island wasn't giving her distance or clarity—it was giving her truth. And that truth had a name.

A gust of wind moved across the cedars, rustling the branches with a voice that felt older than any of them. The path dipped as they stepped into the outskirts of the abandoned village. The air cooled sharply, carrying the scent of weathered wood and something like memory.

Boone adjusted his pack with a grunt. Sadie glanced back and gave him a small smile—gentle, grounding. Boone didn't understand what he sensed between them, but Sadie's compassion reassured him. Jesse's steady presence reassured him too. He didn't know what was shifting; he only knew he wasn't being left behind.

Still... something was there. Something subtle. Something unspoken.

They continued walking. Scout trotted ahead, tail steady, ears perked toward the church.

Sadie's breath caught softly. Everything in her life had felt complicated before this trip—choices, histories, expectations. But something about Jesse... something about the island... something about the two of them standing in old rooms filled with stories... it all whispered of a future she had never dared to imagine.

What if this wasn't an accident?

What if they were meant to find this together?

Jesse felt the same truth rising inside him—quiet but solid.

He wasn't ready to speak it.

Neither was she.

But the island seemed to know.

The path straightened, and the village gathered itself from the dusk—ruins standing in quiet testimony to the lives that once moved here. Porches sagged gently. Windows blinked hollow and dark. The breeze pressed against weathered siding and moved through abandoned doorframes.

Ahead, the pale church steeple lifted into the darkening sky—still, watchful, ancient.

The three friends moved toward it—small silhouettes crossing a vast, remembering landscape.

Chapter Seven

The Old Church

Dusk settled over Portsmouth Village—a soft wash of gold dissolving into violet, the last warm breath of daylight easing across the abandoned field.

Sadie felt it first—a stillness that pressed against her chest like a held breath. She slowed without meaning to.

The evening light was gentle but fading fast, sinking behind the trees. Tall grass bowed in the cooling wind, whispering in long, slow waves that carried faint echoes from a past no living person could recall. Sand, dry on top and cool beneath, shifted in faint ripples where earlier footprints had already begun to blur.

The entire village seemed to watch as the three travelers crossed the grassy field toward the church. Old foundations, skeletons of vanished homes, leaning cedar, and aging fences all seemed to tilt inward as if listening to the slow crunch of their footsteps. In the distance, the rusted pump by an old cistern stood like a forgotten sentinel. Even the air felt reverent—thinner, quieter. Somewhere beyond the dunes, the ocean murmured—a low hush beneath every sound.

Sadie stopped first.

Her breath caught.

"Oh my God... it's beautiful."

Her eyes widened as she spoke. The church—its peeling white paint soft beneath the dusk—held a grace untouched by time. Light clung to its edges, turning its tired lines into something fragile and sacred. The steeple rose modestly against the deepening sky, its silhouette edged in faint gold.

Jesse stepped beside her, eyes narrowing with quiet awe. His shoes sank slightly into the thin crust of sand and grass at the edge of the clearing.

"Looks like a painting."

The church carried a presence that felt older than memory. The warping of the boards, the tilt of the roofline, the worn front steps—decades of weddings, funerals, and ordinary Sundays. He felt the instinctive pull he'd begun to recognize on this island—something unseen, watching, weighing, remembering.

The photograph from the Life-Saving Station flickered behind his eyes—the man who wore his face, staring out from a century ago. Jesse's palms still remembered the phantom weight of oars, the bite of rope, the surge of black water. He hadn't told Sadie everything about that vision.

"Places like this... they hold meaning," he said softly. "Makes you feel like you gotta walk soft, out of respect."

Sadie nodded, the sentiment settling warmly into her chest. The thought of long-ago congregations in their best clothes, of children fidgeting in pews and old men humming along to hymns, flickered through her mind. The church wasn't just a building; it felt like a vessel, still holding every whispered prayer that had ever passed through its doors.

Behind them, Boone shifted, unimpressed. He scraped the sole of his shoe against a buried root and studied the building with a squint.

"Looks like termites and splinters to me."

But even he lingered longer than he intended, something about the building tugging at him despite himself. His eyes traced the warped boards, the silent belfry, the edges worn by salt and storms—not with awe, but with a wary caution he didn't understand.

Scout trotted a few steps ahead, then circled back, ears perked, nose twitching at scents sewn into the wood and sand—old cedar, dust, and the faint, sweet ghost of something floral.

They climbed the porch steps. Jesse wrapped his hand around the iron latch—cool, stiff, textured by salt—and pushed. The hinges answered with a long, weary groan.

For a heartbeat, all three stood still, framed in the doorway, letting their eyes adjust to the shadowed interior.

Then Jesse stepped inside.

The dusk behind them fell away like a dropped curtain. Inside, the air was thick with the scent of old hymnals and long-settled dust, underscored by a faint trace of salt that storms had once slipped through the seams. Time had layered itself into the wood—summers of heat, winters of cold, decades of storms that rattled these walls.

Antique windows warped the last of the day's light into streaks of dull gold across narrow pews. The slanted rays fell in soft ribbons, catching dust that drifted like suspended stars. Spiderwebs clung to the corners of the windows and rafters, delicate lacework that no one had disturbed in years.

"Whoa... It's dark in here," Jesse whispered.

His voice was swallowed instantly, carried upward into rafters that felt impossibly high—a space shaped for sound but holding only silence now.

Sadie pointed into the shadows.

"Look, there are candles. There—and over there."

Her finger traced small glints of glass along the side walls and near the pulpit, shapes barely catching the weak light. Their footsteps echoed softly, a delicate percussion against the hollow boards. Dust shivered in the twilight, shimmering in thin threads where the dim light found it. Somewhere in the distance, a nail shifted within a beam—a tiny, solitary tick.

They struck matches.

One flame.

Then another.

Each caught with a small gasp of gold. Warmth spread outward in trembling halos, painting the pews in gentle amber and setting the edges of the hymnals aglow.

Sadie turned in a slow circle, voice just above a whisper.

"I can't believe this still exists."

Awe. Gratitude. Something deeper she didn't have a name for. She imagined women in Sunday dresses straightening the same lamps, men adjusting their jackets, children urged to sit still. The thought that so much life had happened here, and then simply stopped, made her throat tighten.

"Feels like time is standing still," Jesse murmured, running his fingers along the smooth ridge of a pew. The wood was cool, worn from years of devotion, the varnish dulled by countless hands and kneeling bodies. Something in this place made him feel watched—but not unwelcome. More like he'd stepped into someone else's well-kept memory.

Scout padded quietly between the pews, paws soft on old boards. Her nose lifted toward scents half-buried in time — dust, old paper, faint sweetness of forgotten flowers. She moved gently, as though respecting something invisible, pausing now and then to sniff at the base of a pew or glance up toward the altar.

Sadie's eyes lifted to a faded portrait of Jesus above the pulpit, slightly askew yet calm, enduring. Cracked paint, water streaks, muted tones—and still that expression of gentle resolve. As if the church had kept it safe through decades of wind and solitude, refusing to let it fall. The muted gaze seemed to follow the room—just present.

"Someone brought this all the way out here... and put it right up front where everyone could see it."

Her voice carried a quiet wonder.

Jesse exhaled, the glow from the candles warming his face.

"I remember as a kid, my grandfather—my dad's father—saying that when two or three are gathered together in the Lord's name, He is in the midst of them. I feel that here."

The words settled into the room like they belonged there, like they had been spoken before. Sadie's chest tightened—not from fear, but from something solemn and grounding.

Jesse touched the pedal of the pump organ. The bellows groaned—a long, ancient exhale, stirring dust in the air and waking a faint echo from the rafters.

"Bet they played hymns in here," he whispered. "And showed up even during storms. Whole church must've shaken during the wind."

He imagined sheets of rain slashing against the windows, the congregation huddled together in their Sunday best while the organ wheezed out a hymn that rose above the roar.

Sadie moved to the altar. Her fingers grazed the wood—scratched, worn, but sturdy. Wax drips near the edge—candles once lit for Christmases, funerals, revivals. A tarnished collection plate sat waiting, still holding folded bills left by visitors. The paper had curled slightly at the edges, softened by humidity and time.

Jesse picked it up.

"Look at all the money in here. The tourists must leave something when they visit."

Bills, tens and twenties and a few fives, lay alongside coins that had darkened and dulled. It was a small offering, but it felt heavier than the amount — a quiet promise from people who didn't want the place to be forgotten.

"Like keeping the church alive... in their own way," Sadie said softly.

Jesse slipped two bills of his own inside, smoothing them down with his thumb as if they might straighten out the years themselves.

Sadie smiled at him — soft, genuine.

"You've got a good heart, Jesse."

He glanced away, embarrassed by the praise. But it warmed him all the same. He shifted his weight from one foot to the other, suddenly aware of how close they stood in the lamplight. Boone lingered at the shadows' edge, caught between light and dark—uncertainty flickering across his face.

Sadie inhaled deeply.

"I know we have to go... but I don't want to."

The sanctuary had softened something inside her — a restless ache she hadn't even known she carried. The idea of stepping back out into the exposed field felt strangely harsh now, like walking away from a conversation she hadn't finished.

"It feels like somebody was just here," she whispered.

"Like we're walking in on whatever they left behind."

She pictured a small congregation dispersing only hours ago, hymnals closing, footsteps echoing down the aisle. The air still felt used, as if a final "amen" still hovered there, reluctant to fade.

Jesse nodded.

"Yeah. I'll blow out the candles."

His hand hesitated by the nearest for just a heartbeat, not wanting to give the room back to the dark.

Boone's voice came low from the back of the room.

"Y'all go on — I'll meet you outside."

"You sure?" Jesse asked, turning slightly to see him outlined in the half-shadow of the rear pews.

"Yeah. Last one out."

There was a note in Boone's voice — something he tried to flatten into indifference — that didn't quite match his eyes.

"Thanks, Boone," Sadie said gently.

Jesse, Sadie, and Scout stepped outside. The wooden door sighed shut behind them, wood rubbing against wood in a tired, familiar way, leaving Boone alone in the trembling glow.

The sanctuary felt different the moment the others were gone—larger, emptier, its silence stretched thin. Boone stood still while the lamps flickered, the flames wavering as though agitated by something unseen. Without Jesse's low voice or Sadie's soft questions, the room's stillness pressed harder.

His eyes drifted to the door.

Then to the money.

Jesse had dropped those bills without a second thought. The way people did when money was just paper, not the difference between eating and not eating. Boone's truck needed a fuel pump. His rent was three weeks late. And here sat more cash than he'd clear in two days of framing houses—just sitting there, curling in the humidity, waiting for nobody.

The collection plate sat where Jesse had left it, the folded bills catching the light in a quiet, tempting pile. Boone's jaw tightened. A faint stab of guilt pricked him—sharp, brief—but he swallowed it quickly.

His eyes flicked toward the door. Still closed. No footsteps outside. He was alone.

He looked back at the money. Boone's jaw clenched.

His hand moved toward the plate. Stopped. His fingers hovered there, trembling slightly in the lamplight.

Nobody would know. The church had been empty for decades. The money would just sit here, curling in the humidity, fading into nothing. He'd use it. He needed it. That made it right—didn't it?

His hand closed over the bills.

Boone Allen, you were raised better than this.

"I need it more than they do," he muttered.

His voice sounded wrong in the room, louder than it should have been. He reached down and slid the handful of bills into his pocket. The paper rasped against his fingers, soft and worn, the weight of it suddenly heavier than it had looked on the plate.

The moment he touched the money, a breeze swept through the sanctuary.

"What the—"

The candles quivered. Flames bent sharply, shrinking toward the wicks. Goosebumps lifted along Boone's arms. The temperature seemed to drop in a single, invisible step.

The money in his pocket felt wrong—not just heavy, but hot, like it was burning through the fabric. He pressed his palm against it, but the sensation only deepened.

The shadows in the corners moved. Not drifting—moving. Leaning inward, reaching across the floor toward where he stood. Boone's breath shortened. He told himself it was the candles flickering, playing tricks. But the light was steady now, the flames small and still, and the shadows kept shifting anyway.

A board creaked behind him.

He spun.

Nothing there. Just the portrait of Jesus above the pulpit, dim in the fading light. But the eyes—Boone could swear the eyes were looking at him now. Not painted-looking. Actually looking. The muted gaze that had seemed so gentle earlier felt different now—steady, patient, unblinking. Waiting for him to understand what he'd done.

His chest tightened. His throat felt thick. He knew, suddenly and completely, that he shouldn't have taken the money. Not here. Not from this place.

But his pride flared hot and fast, swallowing the guilt before it could take root. He wasn't putting it back. He wasn't going to stand here and let some old building make him feel small.

He blew out the first candle.

WHOOMPH.

The sound was small but felt too loud, like striking a match in a mausoleum.

Then the second.

WHOOMPH.

The darkness rolled in thicker with each extinguished flame, shadows knitting themselves back together around the pews.

The third flame flickered wildly, almost resisting. It stretched and snapped, thin and frantic, as if trying to cling to the wick.

He leaned in—

WHOOMPH.

Darkness collapsed around him—total, absolute. Only the faintest wash of dying twilight pressed through the warped glass, casting a single crooked stripe across the floor. The air turned cold, tight, pressing against his skin like a held breath.

Boone stood frozen.

The silence wasn't empty. It felt full—dense with something he couldn't name but could feel in his bones.

For one wild, irrational heartbeat, he thought about pulling the money back out of his pocket. Putting it back on the plate. Apologizing to the empty room, to the portrait he could no longer see, to whatever presence lingered in the rafters.

But his pride locked tight around the thought.

He needed to get out. Now.

His pulse hammered as he moved toward the door, footsteps too loud in the hollow silence. Each board creaked beneath him like an accusation. He didn't look back—didn't let himself—but he felt the room behind him anyway, watching his retreat with something that might have been disappointment. Or patience.

His fingers found the latch, clumsy with urgency, and yanked it open.

***

Twilight had deepened into a rich blue, the final threads of daylight slipping behind the dunes. The sky above the village held onto a lingering band of pale gold near the horizon, fading slowly into indigo. A faint breeze drifted across the clearing, carrying the smell of marsh and distant salt water, and the first stars fought their way through the thinning light.

The door eased closed behind them with a soft wooden sigh, leaving Jesse and Sadie alone on the church porch as Scout settled quietly at their feet. The boards beneath them still held the warmth of the day, but the air around them had cooled, wrapping softly over their skin like a light shawl. Evening gathered over the village in a gentle blue hush, fireflies drifting near the grass line. Crickets tuned up along the edges of the field, their steady chorus rising as the light fell.

A quiet awareness passed between them—this was the first time they had been alone since the moment they shared in the cupola, when they had stood so close they could feel each other breathe, almost drawn into something neither of them had been ready to name. The memory hovered between them now, as tangible as the rough wood at their backs.

Jesse's chest ached with everything he wasn't saying. Twelve years. He'd carried this feeling for twelve years—since the summer they were kids and she'd pulled him from the French Broad after the canoe flipped, her hands gripping his arms, her face so close he could count the water droplets on her eyelashes. He'd known then. Known and never said. And now time was running out—the teaching job, the decision, the life waiting to claim him if he didn't choose something else. Choose her.

Sadie's eyes lifted to Jesse, her voice quiet, almost hesitant.

"Places like this... they make you think about what matters. What you'd want. Someday."

She didn't finish the thought, but it hung there between them anyway.

Jesse absorbed the words, something warm stirring beneath his ribs. He stepped closer—not much, just enough—and brushed a loose strand of hair gently away from her face. The touch was careful, unhurried. Her hair caught briefly on his fingers, soft and familiar, and he let his hand drop slowly.

Sadie's skin tingled where his fingers had passed. She wanted to lean into him—to close the distance that had felt unbearable since the cupola. To say I think I've always known. But Boone was inside. The moment wasn't theirs alone. So she held still, letting the almost-touch say what words couldn't yet.

"Yeah," he said quietly. "I know what you mean."

It wasn't much. But the way he said it—low, steady, certain—made it feel like more.

Sadie's breath softened. She glanced briefly toward the now-closed church door, then back at Jesse. The strange, steady comfort he gave her settled around her shoulders like a weight she didn't mind carrying.

"What we felt today..." she started, then stopped.

Jesse nodded, his eyes holding hers. "I felt it too."

The cupola. The height. The view. The almost-kiss. It all compressed into the space between them, thick and undeniable.

"I don't know where this goes," she whispered.

"Me neither."

His throat tightened. The real words pressed against his teeth—I've loved you since we were twelve—but they stayed locked there, too heavy to release. Not yet. Not with Boone inside.

"But I'm not scared of finding out," he said instead.

His hand rested on the railing, inches from hers. Not reaching. Not closing the gap. Just there.

Sadie's fingers shifted slightly, brushing his knuckles. The contact sent a warm current up his arm. Neither of them moved to take it further. The moment settled between them, warm and uncertain.

Scout lifted her head, sniffed the air as if testing it, then eased back down at their feet.

Then—

The wooden door behind them creaked sharply.

Boone stepped out — pale, rattled, shaken. His eyes swept over them quickly, as if checking how long he'd been gone and whether they'd noticed anything he didn't want to explain. The candlelight from inside had left his pupils wide, and the cooler air outside raised a fine chill on his skin.

Sadie wrapped her arms around herself, still carrying the warmth the sanctuary had placed inside her.

"Thank you both so much for coming to the church with me," she said, voice soft. "It means more than you know."

"Wouldn't have missed it," Jesse said.

But even as he spoke, something was off—a tightness around Boone's eyes, the way his shoulders hovered just a bit higher than usual. Scout's ears twitched in his direction, nose flaring as if catching some shift in the air.

"You alright? You look like you saw something."

Before Boone could answer, Sadie brushed his arm, frowning as she noticed him flinch slightly at her touch.

A faint hum rose around them.

Then—suddenly—a thick cloud of mosquitoes engulfed Boone.

They clung to his skin in frenzied swarms, crawling along his neck, arms, face — biting with a kind of targeted violence. The sound of their wings filled the small space between them, a high, insistent whine that seemed to coil around Boone more than anyone else on the porch.

"My God—! What the hell!? Damn things are eating me alive!"

He slapped at his arms and neck, stepping backward off the porch as if trying to walk out of the cloud. The bugs only followed, maddeningly persistent.

Jesse brushed one from his brow.

"They're not that bad."

He glanced down, finding only a couple of lazy stragglers on his own arm. The disparity made his skin prickle.

Sadie flicked another from her ankle.

"I guess they're worse for some people. They must not like you, Boone."

She spoke lightly, but the oddness of it wasn't lost on her. The insects seemed focused, swarming Boone with an almost deliberate ferocity.

"This is insane!"

Boone's voice cracked slightly as he swatted at his neck again, leaving a faint smear where one had already bitten.

Scout growled low, eyes fixed not on the insects but on Boone—and then on the church behind him. Her hackles lifted just slightly. The fur along her spine rippled as she held that line of sight, watching the doorway and Boone.

"Let's get moving," Jesse said. "We've got maybe twenty minutes of light left."

He cast a look toward the western sky, where the last streaks of color were sinking fast. The idea of staying this close to the church, with Boone jittering and the mosquitoes behaving like that, suddenly felt wrong.

"Should we camp by the station?" Sadie asked.

"Yeah. It's closer to the beach and less mosquitos."

They walked across the field, the last scraps of daylight stretching their shadows long, smearing them over the grass and old foundations. The wind shifted lightly, bringing a faint roar from the unseen ocean, the rhythmic crash of waves reminding them how small the island really was.

Boone trailed behind, still swatting at the relentless swarm. A few stragglers clung to his ears and the back of his neck, refusing to give up their hold even as he cursed under his breath and brushed at them with increasing agitation.

Sadie leaned toward Jesse, voice barely above a whisper.

"I think he made someone mad in there."

Her words fluttered into the dark.

"Or something," Jesse replied.

His unease deepened—a quiet, undeniable feeling that whatever Boone had stirred inside that sanctuary wasn't finished with them.

The church faded into the gathering dark behind them—swallowed by shadow, yet somehow still watching.

And deep in the sanctuary, in the darkness Boone had left behind, the air settled slowly back into place—carrying the memory of what had been taken, holding it the way the island held everything: patiently, completely, until the debt came due.

Chapter Eight

The Campfire

Night settled heavy over Portsmouth Island — a vast, ancient hush draped across dunes, marsh, and sound. The moon wasn't up yet and the sky was as black as deep water, scattered with a sharp spray of stars that shimmered like shattered ice. Out here, the darkness didn't simply fall; it claimed the island, saturating every hollow in the dunes and pooling in the creases of the marsh until it felt older than anything human hands had ever built. A cool breath moved across the marsh grass and rippled it like fur, carrying the salt-stung scent of Pamlico Sound. Even the air felt ancestral. Like it had blown across these sands a thousand years before any of them were born and would still be blowing long after they were gone.

Their campsite glowed like a small ember in that endless dark — fragile, temporary, hopeful. Three small tents curved in a loose crescent around the fire, huddled like bright islands in a sea of shadow. Their nylon walls shifted and whispered each time the breeze slid across them, as if the tents were breathing quietly along with the night. When Boone shifted, one of the tent flaps fluttered in response, a soft canvas heartbeat. Sparks drifted upward from the fire with every gust, rising in delicate spirals before being swallowed by the immensity of the darkness above. It was impossible not to feel small beneath that sky.

Nearby, the old Life-Saving Station stood in silhouette — its weathered boards and steep lines cut sharply against the glow of the fire. Even in darkness, the building carried an unmistakable presence, a shape carved from memory rather than wood. It looked as if it had been standing there not for decades, but for centuries, watching storms make and unmake the shoreline, watching people arrive and disappear, watching the tide remain faithful to its purpose while everything else changed. Tonight, its shadowed windows reflected nothing, but the building still seemed awake.

Scout lay curled at Sadie's feet, her body stretched long and warm against the sand. The dog's breathing came in soft, shallow waves — the kind of rest that wasn't rest at all. Her ears twitched every few seconds, responding to some sound the humans couldn't hear: the rustle of a ghost crab, the subtle shift of wind against dune grass, the distant thump of a wave folding against the shore. Scout's tail flicked once, then stilled, but her eyes never fully closed.

Boone sat closest to the flames, his shoes dug into the sand as if bracing himself against something he couldn't name. He poked at the coals with a stick, each jab quick and impatient. Every motion seemed to carry a simmering agitation, like he was stabbing at something inside himself rather than tending the fire. His shoulders were tight, his breath short, the muscles in his jaw shifting.

Jesse reclined on his elbows, stretching his legs toward the heat. The warmth seeped slowly into him, loosening the tension that had lived in his bones since they'd crossed the inlet. He hadn't realized how rigid he'd been until the fire coaxed his body into easing. Sand clung to the backs of his arms and the fabric of his jeans, grounding him in the physical moment while his mind drifted through every unspoken thing that still hovered around them.

Sadie cupped a warm metal mug between her palms. The firelight glinted along its rim, sending small yellow reflections sliding across her fingers. She lifted the mug slowly now and again, inhaling the faint aroma of the drink more often than she actually sipped it. Her shoulders rose and fell with the steadiness of someone trying to stay anchored — not from fear, but from the anticipation of something unnamed.

Boone muttered, low and angry, "I should've kicked that guy's ass."

The words hit the air like a stone dropped in still water. Sadie's gaze drifted toward him, her expression half-curious, half-weary.

"Who—Caleb?" she asked.

Boone shoved the stick deeper into the coals. A spray of sparks jumped upward like startled fireflies.

"Yeah. Ferry boy. Thinks he's hot shit."

Jesse's grin rose slowly, even though he didn't lift his head from his relaxed sprawl.

"I'm not so sure you could take him, Boone."

Sadie let out a soft laugh — unforced, almost musical.

"Just don't mess up his pretty face."

Boone didn't soften. Didn't even blink. His stare fixed on the flames.

"Would be a pleasure."

At that exact moment, the stick in his hand snapped with a dry crack — a brittle, unexpected sound that echoed louder than it should have. Almost simultaneously, the fire popped sharply, sending a spark jumping toward the sand. Scout jerked upright in a quick, startled motion, eyes wide. After a long second, she settled back down, but the tension stayed in her shoulders. Boone noticed his own flinch and tightened his jaw, embarrassed by his reaction.

"Well," Jesse said lightly, "lucky for us, you didn't get the chance."

Sadie sighed, shifting her weight on the sand until her knee brushed lightly against Scout's fur.

"Can we not talk about fighting right now?"

Boone's voice simmered, low and resentful.

"You both think he could take me."

"That's not what I said," Sadie replied, her tone gentle but firm.

Boone didn't respond. Shadows settled along his cheekbones, deepening the lines that frustration carved there. The firelight caught the edges of his face, exposing something older, more tired beneath the irritation — bruises formed long before tonight. He looked momentarily hollow, the kind of hollow that came from years of being compared to invisible standards he never got to define.

"Let it go," Jesse said softly. "He's not here. We'll probably never see him again."

Sadie reached into her pocket, fingertips brushing the folded edge of Caleb's note. She pulled it out, stitching the numbers into her memory. The paper softening at the corners, carrying a warmth that didn't come from the fire. She tucked the note away, trying to ignore the way her pulse shifted with it.

She didn't know why she'd looked at it again. Didn't know why the numbers felt worth memorizing. Just a feeling—the kind she'd learned not to ignore. Like the island was telling her to hold onto it.

The fire sank lower, embers glowing like half-buried heartbeats beneath the ash. The sound of the ocean drifted across the night — soft, steady, ancient. Waves rolled against the shore with the patience of something unconcerned by human worries. Scout exhaled again, long and slow, her breath a thin plume of fog in the cooling air.

A small joint passed between them, its ember glowing as each inhaled. Smoke curled lazily upward and vanished into the star-soaked blackness, as if the night swallowed it before it had a chance to rise. The warmth deepened, turning their small circle into a fragile refuge against the vastness pressing in.

Boone scratched his arms. Then his neck. Then his legs.

"I'm sufferin', guys," he said. "Damn bugs won't leave me alone."

The scratching didn't help. Nothing helped. The bites weren't the problem—they were just what his hands could reach.

The money sat folded in his pocket, pressing against his thigh like something alive. He could still feel the church watching him. His grandmother's voice, quiet and disappointed: Boone Allen, you were raised better than this.

He scratched harder.

Jesse smirked, rolling slightly to glance at him.

"You sure it's the skeeters bothering you?"

Boone shot him a glare sharp enough to cut.

Sadie leaned back, tilting her head toward the sky. The stars shimmered with a brilliance that almost hurt to look at.

"Look at those stars..."

Jesse followed her gaze, his breath softening.

"You can see everything out here. No light pollution. No noise."

"Makes you feel tiny," Sadie whispered. "But in a good way."

"Like the universe is saying you're not the center of it all," Jesse said.

"Yeah... comforting, somehow."

Scout shifted her weight, nestling closer to Sadie's boots, her warmth anchoring them all.

Boone kept scratching, relentless, frustrated.

"I don't like this place."

Sadie frowned.

"Are you serious? I love it here."

"There's something about it..." Jesse murmured.

He stared toward the marsh. The reeds trembled, but not entirely from wind. There was a quality to their movement — fluid, layered, almost like breath rather than breeze. Jesse felt old memories surface: the last time he'd come here, the quiet that had wrapped around him like a blanket he didn't know he needed.

Sadie nodded, gaze drifting toward the dunes, her eyes reflecting firelight.

"It's like we're being watched — but not in a scary way. Like the island sees us."

The night thickened around them, a soft but intentional hush. Even the fire seemed to draw in its crackles, listening.

Boone snorted.

"That's just the weed messing with your head."

"No," Sadie said quietly. "It's more than that. You feel it?"

Jesse met her eyes — and something passed between them, subtle as the shift of flame.

"Yeah. I do."

The island's attention felt specific—not general presence, but recognition. The way the photograph in the Life-Saving Station had looked at him. Like Portsmouth knew him. Had known him before he arrived. Was waiting to see what he'd choose.

Scout lifted her head again, ears stiff, sensing something none of them could see. Her body sharpened, alert. After a long moment, she eased back down, but her eyes remained half-open, scanning the dark.

Boone clawed at his arms, more aggressively this time.

"I feel like I'm gonna claw my skin off."

Jesse leaned toward Sadie and whispered something too low for Boone to hear. Sadie laughed softly, a sound as gentle as breeze through marsh grass. Jesse laughed too — a quick, nervous exhale he didn't fully intend.

The fire had drawn them closer without asking. Sadie shifted slightly, her shoulder brushing Jesse's in a small, unplanned contact. The moment barely lasted a second — but it was enough.

Jesse felt the contact like a current—accidental, everything. Twelve years of silence pressed against his ribs. The French Broad. The canoe flip. Her face when she came up laughing. He'd known then what he couldn't say.

The Raleigh job could wait. Would wait. Let the deadline pass. Wherever Sadie landed—mountains or coast—that's where he wanted to be.

Tonight could be different. But not with Boone right there, watching.

Boone noticed immediately.

A crack of vulnerability crossed his face before he buried it so fast the firelight barely caught it. Loneliness flickered through him, raw as scraped skin.

"Must be nice... having someone to understand you," he muttered.

He jabbed at the fire too hard. Sparks leapt high, scattered, and vanished into the night.

For the first time all evening, Boone didn't look angry.

He looked alone.

They'd talked about cities, coasts, grad schools—futures that didn't include the mountains. Futures that didn't include him. He'd be the one still there, waving goodbye from the same gravel road.

Sadie broke the silence gently, choosing her words with care.

"So... now that we're actually here... tell me again, Jesse. Why Portsmouth?"

Jesse nudged one of the glowing coals, watching it pulse orange.

"We talked before we left the mountains... and again on the ferry."

"But you never really explained," Sadie said.

Jesse's breath eased out slowly. Firelight carved warm amber across his features.

"The first time I came here, I wasn't in college yet. Didn't know what I wanted — or if I even wanted to go. Everyone had an opinion. None of it felt right."

Sadie's expression softened, her attention fixed on him.

"But coming out here..." Jesse continued, "it quieted everything. Gave me space to hear myself."

"Is that when you made the choice to go to UNC?" she asked.

"Yeah. Chapel Hill felt right. Something I chose. Not something forced upon me."

"And now you're back... and you have to choose again."

"Pretty much," Jesse said.

Sadie nodded, something crossing her face like light shifting under water.

"I get that. I don't know what I want either. Everyone else seems to know what they're doing, and I'm... trying to catch up."

Jesse looked at her, the firelight catching softly in her eyes.

"Maybe that's why we're all here. Hoping the island helps us find answers."

"Yeah," Sadie whispered. "I'm hoping for that too."

Boone cut in, brittle and sharp.

"Must be nice."

They turned toward him, the shadows shifting.

"Talking about choices and futures..." Boone said. "Some of us don't get that."

"Boone—" Sadie began.

"No," he snapped. "You two can go anywhere. Me? I got one road. Maybe two if I'm lucky."

Sadie softened, voice barely above the crackle of the fire.

"That's not what we meant."

Boone stared deeper into the flames, the reflection bending in his eyes.

"I'll probably die in the same town we were born in. Swinging a shovel or a hammer. Because that's all I got."

Silence washed over them. The fire cracked like punctuation.

"Maybe..." Sadie said carefully, "we should just enjoy this moment. Take in the peace and quiet. Listen to whatever this place has to say."

Boone swallowed, his throat working.

"All I know is I'm afraid of losing y'all. Getting left behind."

Jesse felt guilt tighten like a band around his ribs. Sadie's eyes warmed.

She wanted to tell him he wouldn't lose them. But she wasn't sure it was true.

Scout stretched her legs, nudging her body halfway across Sadie's and Jesse's knees. Boone's gaze lingered on that small closeness, and something inside him hollowed further.

A gust swept the campsite. The flame bent low, trembling in the wind's grip. Sand skittered across the ground in thin streams. Scout snapped upright, muscles taut.

"Wind's picking up," Jesse said quietly.

"Yeah..." Sadie murmured. "It wasn't blowing like this earlier."

Boone rubbed his arms, the shivering motion half from irritation, half from the cooling air.

"Well... maybe this wind'll at least blow the bugs away from me."

Jesse watched the flame as it whipped sideways.

"Weather changes fast out here. We may not make it back tomorrow."

Sadie looked toward the dunes. Her pulse ticked faster.

"Feels like something's coming."

Boone huffed, unwilling to give weight to anything but his own resolve.

"Something may be coming, but I know where I'm going tomorrow. Home."

The wind sharpened, chilly now, threading through their shirts and tugging at loose strands of hair.

The gust died. But another followed seconds later, colder, more insistent.

Embers glowed brighter, responding to the pressure building in the night. Thin clouds slid across the stars, dimming them one by one until the sky felt closer, almost pressing down.

Scout's ears rotated toward the sound—toward the water, the marsh, the dark spaces between. She whined once.

The island breathed — a long, slow exhale across dunes and marsh — and everything in the campsite stilled.

Jesse looked at Sadie across the dying fire. Her face soft in the ember-light, eyes half-closed.

Tomorrow, he thought. I'll tell her tomorrow.

But the island had heard that promise before, from other men who'd run out of time.

Chapter Nine

Storm Morning

Morning arrived without sunlight.

It eased its way across the island as a dull, colorless presence — not a dawn so much as a slow revealing of something unsettled, waiting beyond sight. Shadows lifted only halfway, smearing along the dune lines instead of pulling back clean. The wind had woken first, sweeping through the trees and bushes in restless, uneven gusts, shaking their tents like thin sails straining against a rising tide. Fine sand hissed across the campsite in faint, stinging sheets, brushing over coolers, guy lines, and the half-buried rings of old footprints. The familiar shapes of their little world — packs, shoes, the cold circle of the fire pit — all looked slightly wrong, as if someone had slid a gray film over the island while they slept.

Overhead, thick slabs of gray cloud churned and folded into one another, swallowing whatever colors were meant to greet the morning. The faintest trace of pink or gold never made it through — a flat, bruised wash that turned the dunes the color of bone. The whole sky felt heavy, a warning stretched taut across the horizon — the kind the island whispered before it chose to roar. Far off, beyond the cut of the dune ridge, the ocean's voice had deepened, a low, constant roar that vibrated underneath everything, like a long, held note. It sounded less like background and more like a presence — something awake and paying attention.

Scout sat rigid outside Sadie's tent, a dark shape etched against the pale sand. Her posture was unnervingly still, ears flicking, eyes narrowed, nose lifted toward the shifting currents as though reading messages written into the air. A thin tremor worked through the muscles along her shoulders, not from cold but from tension held too long. She wasn't merely alert — she was interpreting something the others could not yet sense.

The fire pit was nothing but a shallow basin of gray ash and half-charred wood, last night's warmth long gone. Scout's paw prints ringed it in tight circles where she had paced before choosing her spot, and those tracks were already softening, blurred by the wind's steady hand. Her nose twitched once, twice, then again, testing the air as the scent of the sound shifted from briny and familiar to something sharper, colder, edged with salt and the far-off taste of churned-up depths. Somewhere in that shift was a note Jesse and Sadie would never be able to register — but Scout did, and it tightened every line of her body.

Inside his tent, Jesse stirred awake to the groan of canvas and the uneasy moan of wind sliding across the dunes. The nylon walls flexed in and out around him, breathing with the gusts. Before he understood anything consciously, he felt it — the pressure in the air, the way the wind pushed against the thin fabric overhead. Something inside him tightened in response. He'd slept through storms his whole life — mountain storms that rattled windows, summer downpours that slapped the earth like open palms — but this felt different. This wind had purpose. Direction. Intent.

He lay still for one more breath, staring at the faint, shifting shadows above him. The air in the tent smelled like damp nylon, sand, and the faint residue of smoke from his clothes. A grain of sand scratched beneath his cheekbone. Another had somehow found its way into the back of his throat, leaving a dry, gritty taste. As another gust shuddered across the campsite, the tent poles creaked, and a loose zipper tab tapped a nervous rhythm against its metal ring. His chest tightened the way it did right before a basketball tip-off back home — the moment before action, when the world held its breath — only this time, there was no crowd, no scoreboard, no control. Just the sense that something big and indifferent was about to move.

He unzipped his tent as a sudden gust slammed into it, snapping the flap outward and flooding the space with cold, salty air. The canvas whipped hard enough to sting his fingers. Jesse winced at the bite of the chill and blinked through the sting of blown sand and salt. The zipper's teeth rasped loud in his ears, almost swallowed by the constant rush of wind. The noise was a harsh metal rasp cutting through the soft, cotton-thick haze of sleep.

Stepping out, he rubbed warmth into his arms, palms moving over the thin fabric of his sleeves as if he could chase the cold out through friction alone. Goosebumps rose instantly along his skin. The sand beneath his bare feet was cool and damp, the top layer sliding away as he shifted his weight. He flexed his toes, feeling the give and pull of the island under him, the faint suction of moisture just below the surface. He lifted his head, scanning the sky like a sailor trying to read troubled water. The morning light looked wrong — thin, metallic, drained — the kind that didn't just indicate weather but announced it. The horizon line where sea met sky had lost its clean edge, blurred into a smudged band of movement. The whole world seemed to be made of shifting grays.

"Huh... I think we over-slept."

His voice came out softer than he intended, immediately swallowed by the wind. The words felt small out here, like they didn't belong to the same world as the rising sea and racing clouds. His breath blew out in a pale puff and vanished almost instantly, ripped sideways. For a second, he found himself wishing for the simple, dumb problems of a late morning at home — missed alarms, cold cereal — instead of whatever this day was about to be.

Before he could take in much more, Boone exploded from his tent — not stepping out, but tearing out, shoes punching into sand, hands ripping at tent stakes in frantic, uneven bursts. The entire tent lurched with him, one corner collapsing, the fabric twisting like something alive. His movements were jerky, uncoordinated. Panic moved through him like static under the skin. His breath came short and sharp, frayed at the edges.

Boone's hair stuck out in wild, uneven angles, flattened on one side from the pillow and damp with sweat along his temples. Dark half-moons pooled beneath his eyes, turning them hollow. His jaw worked as he yanked at the guy lines, knuckles whitening, fingers shaking as he worked. He looked like someone who had spent the entire night holding something back by sheer will, and that will was almost gone.

The money was still in his pocket—one of a dozen things that had kept him staring at the tent ceiling all night. The church. The inlet. Their futures pulling away from his.

Could the island be punishing him?

He shoved the thought down and kept packing.

A knot gathered in Jesse's gut. He watched Boone for two, three heartbeats, the same way he'd watched him on the inlet the day before — searching for the familiar version of his friend behind the stranger's frantic movements. The Boone he knew talked too loud, laughed easily, made everything feel like an adventure. The Boone in front of him looked like the island had stripped all of that away and left something raw and cornered.

"Hey — you okay?"

The words left Jesse before he fully formed them, instinct pushing them through his teeth. He angled closer, voice raised just enough to cut through the wind without turning into a shout. His hand hovered for a second, wanting to reach out, then dropped back to his side.

"No I'm not okay," Boone barked. "Barely slept a wink last night."

His words were clipped, bitten through with something brittle. He didn't look at Jesse — just kept yanking at the guy lines, fingers shaking as he worked. The stake he ripped free flew sideways and thudded into the sand a few feet away. He didn't notice. Jesse did — the wild, careless throw of it, the way Boone's hands were moving faster than his thoughts, like he was trying to physically outrun the panic that had been chewing at him in the dark.

Sadie crawled from her tent next, hair tousled, sleep still fogging her eyes. The flap sagged around her shoulders as she pushed it aside, and the first slap of cold air made her blink hard. She braced one hand in the sand, letting her other come up to wipe at her face. Grains of sand clung to her palm and smeared across her cheek. She blinked hard into the wind and lifted her face toward the roiling sky. The breeze clawed at her ponytail, ripping free loose strands that lashed against her cheeks. Her expression shifted from confusion to concern, the last remnants of sleep burning off in a single, sharp look upward.

"I was hoping it would be nice today... Is this what they call a Nor'easter?"

Her voice carried a thin line of hope through it, as if naming it might make it less threatening, less unknown. The word itself felt borrowed from Caleb's mouth, from some earlier conversation — a bit of local language she'd tried on because it made this place feel a little more like a story than a threat. Hearing it now, with the sky like this, it didn't feel like a story at all.

Jesse moved beside her, reading the sky with a mix of instinct and dread. He folded his arms across his chest, tucking his hands into his armpits for warmth. The clouds rolled low and fast, their underbellies darkening by the minute, tugged by something far beyond the dunes. The horizon had begun to blur into a smeared, shifting bruise. A distant rumble — not thunder, not yet — murmured at the edge of hearing, like the ocean clearing its throat.

"Don't know," he murmured. "But it ain't looking good."

He kept his eyes on the sky as he spoke, tracking the speed of the clouds, counting the time between gusts without even realizing he was doing it. The wind caught the edge of his shirt and snapped it flat against his ribs. In the mountains, he'd learned to trust the feeling that settled in his chest before a bad storm; here, that feeling was tangled up with the unfamiliar shape of the horizon and the endless flatness of water that had nowhere else to go.

A sudden SLAM cracked from the direction of the Life-Saving Station — a loose shutter snapping backward in a punishing gust. The sound echoed like a gunshot across the dunes. The old building seemed to flinch with it, timbers shuddering, then settling again into their patient lean toward the sea. Sadie flinched sharply, shoulders jerking up toward her ears. Scout growled, low and certain, her paws digging slightly into the sand as she braced herself. The growl vibrated through her chest, a steady note of warning, not bravado.

"Scout doesn't growl at wind," Sadie whispered.

The statement landed heavy. Jesse knew it was true — Scout had instincts older than theirs, sharper than theirs. The hair along the dog's spine lifted as she tracked something moving beyond sight. Her eyes locked on the line of dunes that separated them from the beach, as if there were already a shape there, already a threat, even if they couldn't see it. The island spoke to her in scents and subtle changes of pressure; whatever it was saying now, she didn't like it.

Boone's pace grew more frantic, more erratic, as if he were trying to dismantle the campsite faster than the wind could. He tugged so hard at his pack that the seams protested, the zipper teeth straining. His shoes kept sinking into the soft sand, throwing off his balance and making him look even more unsteady. Twice he staggered, catching himself on the corner of a cooler, muttering under his breath. The curses were half-formed, more air than words.

"Maybe we should wait," Sadie said. "Let this weather pass before we try to cross the inlet again."

She spoke carefully, choosing each word like she was stepping on thin ice. Her eyes never left Boone as she said it, watching the set of his shoulders, the clench of his jaw. She knew him well enough to recognize that this was not just nerves; this was something closer to coming apart.

"No," Boone spat. "I'm not wasting another day out here."

The voice wasn't Boone's — not the Boone who joked his way through discomfort, or the Boone who'd kept his cool inside the church. This voice was tight, cornered, wired with something raw. The refusal cut through the wind like a snapped cable. The island might be wide open in every direction, but Boone sounded like a man trapped in a room with walls closing in.

Jesse stepped closer, steady and calm. He planted his feet wide in the sand so the gusts wouldn't shove him backward and angled his body slightly, trying to put himself in Boone's line of sight without blocking his way. He could feel Sadie behind him, a quiet, worried presence at his shoulder.

"Boone... slow down. You're not yourself this morning. Just talk to me for a second."

Boone yanked a rope hard enough to burn his palm, hissing at the sting but refusing to pause. A thin red line rose across his skin almost instantly. Sand clung to the scraped skin as he shoved his hand against his pack. He flexed his fingers once, shook them out, and went right back to wrestling with the straps. If anything, the pain seemed to fuel him, give him something sharp to focus on that wasn't the storm, wasn't the inlet, wasn't the rising panic in his own thoughts.

"We came across — we'll get back across."

The words came out flat, like something memorized and repeated, a promise he was making more to himself than to them. He wasn't arguing with the weather; he was arguing with the fear that had settled into him the moment the light began to change.

Sadie moved in, worry settling across her features. The wind whipped loose strands of her hair against her cheeks, but she didn't react. Her hands hovered for a second, as if she wanted to reach out and steady him and thought better of it. She could feel Jesse's tension beside her, the way his shoulders had gone rigid beneath his jacket.

"Boone, the inlet is going to be worse... nothing like yesterday."

She glanced toward the dunes as she said it, hearing the surf pounding beyond them, the way it thudded against the shore like fists on a door. Yesterday's crossing replayed itself in her mind in flashes — the heave of the water, the drag of the current — now laid over whatever the sea had turned into overnight.

"It's just wind."

But Scout disagreed.

She paced between them, tail low, ears pinned back, steps hesitant and uneasy. She hovered near Boone, then circled back to Jesse and Sadie — as if deciding who most needed protecting. Each time she passed Boone, she slowed, nudged his leg with her nose, then retreated again, unsettled by the tremor running through him that the others could only see, not smell. She gave a soft, anxious whine once, almost swallowed by the wind, and then cut it off, dropping her head as if bracing for something only she knew was coming.

Sadie looked up again, her voice tightening.

"This doesn't look good. I've got a bad feeling about this."

The feeling wasn't new. It had been building since last night—since she'd studied Caleb's number without knowing why. The island had been trying to tell her something. Now it was shouting.

The words hooked into Jesse, snagging on his own unease. Bad feeling, he thought. The whole island feels like a bad feeling in this moment. He could feel it in the way the wind didn't come in gentle, predictable breaths, but in sharp, uneven surges; in the way the clouds looked less like weather and more like a lid being lowered.

A stronger gust blew through the campsite, shaking the tents and snapping nylon like overworked sails. The sound roared through the air, drowning their breath for a moment. Jesse squinted southeast — clouds rolling in faster, darker, heavier, their edges fraying as they raced across the sky. The Life-Saving Station loomed behind them, a dark, watchful shape, as if the island itself had already written this scene a hundred times and knew exactly how it could go wrong.

"If it gets worse, we could call Caleb—"

Boone froze.

Completely.

He snapped his head toward her, rigid and electric, the wind whipping around him like something alive. His eyes sharpened, fixing on Sadie with a suddenness that made Jesse's stomach drop. The mere sound of Caleb's name seemed to hit something raw and exposed inside him, like pressing on a bruise.

"Are you serious? Absolutely not. We're not calling Caleb."

The name hit something deep in him, turned whatever fear he'd been wrestling into anger. The wind grabbed the words and flung them back at them, harsher, louder. Sadie's shoulders drew in a fraction, more from the intensity of his reaction than from the temperature.

Jesse stepped between the tension. He shifted enough so that Sadie was slightly behind his shoulder, not hidden, but sheltered from the full brunt of Boone's glare. He could feel Boone's stare skate off him, searching for someone to fight that wasn't the storm, wasn't himself.

"We could call one of the small passenger ferries. Or the park service. They always keep someone around—"

"No park service. No ferries. No calls."

Boone's reply snapped out before Jesse even finished, as if he'd been waiting for that suggestion, braced against it all night. He jerked his pack shut with violent urgency. The zipper scraped like a blade, the sound running rough along Jesse's nerves. Every move Boone made had the frantic energy of someone convinced that the only way out was through, no matter what waited on the other side.

"I'm leaving. Now."

Sadie stiffened. A muscle jumped in her cheek. Jesse finally saw it — the truth Boone had been hiding since the church.

Fear.

Not the reasonable kind.

The spiraling, cornered kind.

"You're not even thinking—" Sadie started.

"I have thought," Boone snapped. "All night. And I'm not staying another night on this damn island."

His voice broke slightly on the word "night," not enough to be obvious, but enough that Jesse heard it — the echo of every hour Boone had lain awake, listening to the wind press harder and harder against the thin walls of his tent. In the dark, the island had stretched out endless in every direction, and Boone had been alone with the memory of yesterday and the knowledge that there was only one way back. He slung his pack over his shoulder and stormed toward the dunes — shoes punching deep into the sand, pace reckless, shoulders locked. The trail he left behind was messy, uneven, stamped with more force than direction.

"Boone, this isn't you talking," Sadie said gently, but he didn't turn back.

Scout barked once — sharp and alarmed — watching him vanish over the rise as if she knew the world beyond it was about to change shape. The bark bounced off the wooden bones of the Life-Saving Station and came back thinner, carried away by the wind. For a heartbeat, Sadie thought Boone might stop, might at least hesitate at the sound. He didn't.

Sadie stared after him.

"He's really doing it..."

Her voice was small, the words more breath than sound. She could feel her pulse thudding in her throat, an uneven beat that seemed to sync with the crash of the surf beyond the dunes.

"Yeah," Jesse said quietly. "And if he reaches that inlet alone... I'm not sure he won't leave without us."

The thought came out of him before he could soften it. He could see Boone's back already in his mind, hunched against the wind on the shoreline, the johnboat shoved into foaming water, oars biting into the chop with a desperate, stubborn rhythm. Boone disappearing into that gray distance while they stood on the sand, too late.

Sadie dropped to her pack, hands moving quickly, though a tremor pulsed beneath her movements. The zipper snagged once and she forced herself to breathe, to slow just enough to free it instead of tearing it. Her fingers felt clumsy, slightly numb from the cold wind and from the rush of adrenaline in her veins. Jesse followed, his fingers stiff with cold and urgency. The straps felt awkward under his hands, as if the air itself were thickening around them, trying to slow them down. Scout sprinted ahead, circled back, then bolted forward again — her instincts more insistent by the second, like she could feel every second they wasted ticking away.

"Jesse — if he tries to cross alone... he could die out there."

The words lodged in the space between them, stark and bare. Jesse heard the raw truth in them and didn't try to deflect it. The image flashed again — Boone in the channel, the inlet closing over him, the storm finishing what fear had started. The realization pinched something deep in his chest.

"I know. We need to catch him before he gets to the boats."

He shrugged his pack on, the weight of it settling across his shoulders like a decision. Whatever the storm was going to do, whatever Boone was going to do, they couldn't meet it standing still.

Another hard gust rattled the tents to their cores. Fabric strained, poles shuddered, sand whipped across their shoes in biting sheets. The world felt thinner, less stable — as if the island itself were bracing. The shutter on the Life-Saving Station slammed again, a hollow, warning clap. One of the abandoned guy lines snapped loose and thrashed in the wind like something trying to escape.

"Should we call someone?" Sadie asked. "Caleb? The park service? Anyone?"

Her voice rose just enough to be heard above the wind, but not enough that it felt like a cry for help. Part of her wanted nothing more than to hear Caleb's calm, familiar voice cut through this rising chaos. Another part knew how Boone would react, how thin the wire he was walking really was.

"Not yet," Jesse said. "If he finds out we called for help, he'll lose it completely. Let's try to stop him first."

He imagined Boone hearing Caleb's name again over the wind, imagined the explosion that would follow. Right now, getting to him felt like walking out on a narrow ledge — one wrong move and he'd jump. He swallowed hard, tasting salt and something metallic at the back of his tongue.

Sadie swung her pack over her shoulders. The straps bit in immediately, but she barely felt it. The wind sliced colder across the dunes, carrying the bite of something rising fast offshore. The air had that strange, charged quality storms brought — as if every grain of sand were holding its own static. Her heart was beating too fast, but she pushed that aside, focusing instead on the solid weight of her pack, the familiar sound of Scout's tags chiming softly as the dog trotted ahead.

"We need to move. He's already ahead."

"Let's go."

They hurried toward the narrow trail leading to the beach. The sand there had been packed down by their feet the day before, but overnight the wind had begun to erase those paths, filling them, softening them, making each step sink deeper. It felt like walking across something the island was trying to reclaim. Scout darted ahead, paused, waited, then sprinted forward again — urging them on. Her paws kicked up little bursts of sand that were snatched away before they landed.

The sand shifted unpredictably underfoot, dragged by the early fingers of the incoming tide. Jesse felt it in his bones — the ocean was louder than it should've been. Closer than it should've been. Angrier. The roar of the surf rolled over the dune line like the sound of a crowd heard from outside a stadium — constant, pulsing, impossible to ignore. Each step they took seemed to sink into that sound, pull them toward it.

Above them, the sky pressed lower, tightening, darkening with every breath. The clouds moved in bands, layered and relentless, like the island was being roofed over in gray. A faint, metallic tang sharpened on the air, the smell that came right before rain and lightning and things breaking loose.

The surf thundered inland — louder and closer than it should have been from this distance.

A warning.

A promise.

The island turning from patient to primal.

"If we can't catch him at the inlet..." Jesse murmured.

He pictured Boone standing at the water's edge, shoulders hunched, jaw clenched, making the worst decision of his life in the space of a single breath. For the first time since they'd stepped onto the ferry days ago, Jesse felt the island as something that could take, not just show.

"God help him."

They ran toward the sound of the rising sea. The wind knifed into their faces, snatching at their clothes and packs, but they leaned into it, driven by something sharper than fear. Scout streaked ahead, a dark blur against the pale sand, racing toward the place where sky, sea, and danger were already colliding. Whatever waited at the inlet, the island was done whispering. It was raising its voice now.

Chapter Ten

The Inlet

The wind had not simply risen overnight — it had awakened. It had become a violent thing that had waited patiently for the sun to rise so it could reveal how angry it was. Its howl skated low across the sand like a living warning, each new gust gathering strength as though feeding on the island itself. By midday, it tore across Portsmouth Island like something long denied, reclaiming the land with a force that felt almost personal. The air tasted of raw salt, sharp enough to sting the tongue, as if the storm had scraped its way across miles of open water and arrived hungering for more.

The sky churned overhead with a bruised, grayish-violet sheen, deepening near the horizon where clouds twisted into uneven, unnatural layers. Those layers moved in jagged, convulsive motions, shifting like muscle beneath skin, giving the entire sky a disturbed, living quality. The light filtering through them looked sickly and metallic, stripped of warmth. Even shadows behaved strangely, stretching in broken angles as the changing light cut across the landscape in stuttering pulses. Sand lifted in wide, shimmering sweeps, rolling and curling like smoke before lashing sideways across the beach. Each gust hurled stinging grains against their faces and arms, as if the island itself had grown tired of tolerating their presence. The grains hit with needle-like precision, tiny sparks of pain that accumulated into a raw burn across exposed skin.

The tide hammered the shoreline with straight on fury. Waves crashed, slanting across the sand in violent bursts that sent sheets of foam spiraling upward. The foam twisted in midair like torn fabric, flung skyward before being shredded apart by the next gust. Some pieces dissolved before ever touching the ground; others clung briefly to dune grass before the wind reclaimed them. The surf no longer moved with rhythm — it lurched and staggered, a heartbeat slipping off its natural pattern. Every breaker seemed to arrive prematurely or too late, crashing in unpredictable fits that made the shoreline feel unstable and alive. The sound of the ocean had changed too; it no longer roared but snarled, a guttural, uneven bellow that seemed to rise from the earth itself.

Jesse leaned into the gale with Sadie close behind him, both bent at the waist, bracing each step like climbers scaling a trembling mountain ridge. Their shoes sank and slid in shifting sheets of sand, the ground rolling underfoot as though the beach were trying to shrug them off. The sand behaved like water beneath their shoes, shifting in restless ripples, never holding form long enough to trust. Each uneven step forced their muscles into constant adjustment, a never-ending fight to stay upright. The cold gnawed at their legs through wet fabric, and every inhale scraped their throats raw.

Scout darted ahead in urgent bursts, then circled back with frantic energy, her entire posture vibrating with warning. Her ears pinned flat, her tail low, her movements sharp and insistent. She felt the storm in her bones — not just the weather but the shift in the island's mood, the pulse of something ancient stirring. Her paws dug trenches in the sand as she braced against gusts, shaking her head as if trying to clear the storm from inside her skull. Even her bark, when it came, was swallowed almost instantly by the wind's roar.

They finally spotted Boone near the john boat — a solitary figure locked in battle with the storm. The wind clawed at his jacket, snapping it violently against his ribs, twisting the straps of his pack as if trying to peel them from his shoulders. His movements were frantic, jerky. He shoved gear into the boat with a force that made the hull shudder. Fear lived in every gesture. His breath burst out in quick, uneven clouds, ripped away instantly, as though even his fear could not linger long in the open air. His eyes darted between the boat, the inlet, and the swirling sky, as if trying to measure a path through something that refused to be measured.

"Boone! Stop! Just stop a second!" Sadie shouted, though the wind nearly tore the words from her mouth.

Boone didn't turn.

"I told you — I'm going!"

His voice cracked under the roar, the wind shredding the ends of his words.

"Boone, we are NOT letting you cross that inlet alone!" Jesse yelled.

Boone spun around. His eyes were wild. He looked like a man cornered by more than weather.

"Try and stop me!"

The waves were crashing behind them, rhythmic bursts that sent spray flying across their backs like shattered glass. Sadie raised her arm defensively, blinking against the sting. Cold droplets clung to her hair and lashes before the wind stripped them away. The taste of brine hit her tongue, bitter and cold. Her breath caught as the water soaked through the fabric at her shoulders, chilling instantly against her skin. Jesse wiped a sleeve across his face, though the gesture was useless — the storm plastered new water against him faster than he could clear the old.

"Please! Think about what you're doing!" she cried.

A rare lull in the wind let her voice slip through clearly.

Boone hesitated — only for a heartbeat — but enough for doubt to break through the storm's hold on him. He jerked his head toward the dunes.

"Fine! Let's go up there! Talk where we don't have to scream!"

Relief flickered between Jesse and Sadie.

They followed him up into the dunes, Scout racing ahead, glancing back repeatedly to make sure they were close. Her paws kicked up thin trails of sand that vanished instantly, devoured by the wind. Boone climbed unevenly, shoulders tight, breaths harsh and fast. Jesse noticed the tremor in his hands.

Ducking in behind the dunes gave them only the slightest shelter, but even that felt like a reprieve. The full-throated scream of the wind softened into a lower, relentless push. Sea oats flattened nearly to the ground, their long blades snapping back and forth. Sand clung to their jackets, hair, and lashes, gathering in gritty seams of fabric. Breathing became easier in the small wind break, though the air still vibrated with tension, the storm's undertone humming through their chests like distant thunder.

They sank onto a patch of flattened sand nestled between two ridges. The hollow trapped pockets of cold air, swirling around them in a muted echo of the chaos above. Scout curled between them, body tense, ears flicking with every shift of sound. Her fur ruffled in sharp bursts whenever the wind tunneled through the dunes, but she stayed pressed close, sensing the emotional storm brewing just as fiercely as the physical one. Boone rubbed his palms against his knees, the motion restless, jittery, betraying the exhaustion he was trying to hide.

For a moment, none of them spoke. Storm silence carried a weight.

"Boone... we all slept in later than we should've this morning," Sadie said softly.

Her voice trembled. Boone lifted his eyes to hers. His shoulders sagged a fraction, as though simply hearing her voice loosened something he had been holding rigid inside himself.

"And it took us hours to get down the beach," she added. "It's already midday."

Boone's breathing quickened. Scout nudged his hand, pressing her cold nose against his skin. Boone pulled away as though the touch burned —

not rejecting her, but fighting the unraveling it triggered. He dragged in a sharp breath, eyes shining with a mixture of panic and stubbornness.

"We've got four... maybe five hours of daylight left," Sadie whispered. "If anything slows us down—"

Her voice faltered.

"We won't make it before dark."

The truth fell between them like lead.

Jesse leaned forward, elbows braced on his knees. His voice came low, steady — not because he felt steady, but because someone had to anchor the moment. The wind tugged at his hair.

"Boone... just listen for a second."

Boone stared at the sand, jaw tight.

"If the tide turns while we're in that inlet—"

Jesse let the silence complete the sentence. Deadly. Unforgiving. Final.

Scout whimpered softly pressing closer to Boone's leg.

"This isn't a normal tide," Jesse continued, voice dropping. "It's a King Tide."

Sadie inhaled sharply. The words hit like a cold blade.

"King Tides run harder," Jesse said. "They turn faster. And with a nor'easter blowing across the inlet—"

"If the tide turns, there's no fighting it."

Boone shot back.

"You think I don't know that?! It's a King Tide — yeah — and that current's ripping toward Ocracoke right now. Pushing inshore. That's what's gonna help us beat the wind."

"Boone... we can't be sure," Jesse said quietly.

Boone swallowed.

"Right now, the tide helps," Jesse said. "But when a King Tide turns—"

"It'll turn with a vengeance," Sadie whispered.

Her voice trembled.

Boone's gaze flicked between them, something cracking open behind his eyes.

"Boone... I don't want to lose you... either of you," Sadie said.

The words landed like a blow.

Boone flinched — visibly, painfully.

The dunes seemed to still. Even the wind hesitated.

Boone's voice came out barely above a whisper, raw as an open wound.

"You talk about losing... I can't lose you two."

Sadie covered her mouth as tears filled her eyes, drying almost instantly in the wind. Jesse dropped his gaze, unable to look at Boone without feeling something twist in him.

Scout leaned firmly against Boone's leg, anchoring him.

"I can't be the one left behind," Boone whispered. "I can't stay up there in the mountains all alone while you two figure out your lives somewhere else. I can't—"

His voice broke. The wind filled the space where words should have been.

"You ain't the only one," Jesse said softly. "I'm scared of the same damn thing. Being in the city by myself. While y'all live the good life in the mountains back home."

For a single heartbeat, everything stilled. Wind paused. Sand stopped swirling. Clouds hung suspended. As if the storm itself held breath with them.

Then Boone surged to his feet. He stepped out of the protective hollow — and the storm attacked. Wind detonated across the beach, slamming into them with brutal force. Sadie staggered backward a step. Surf boomed like thunder. Sand ripped across the dunes in violent bursts, stinging their skin. Jesse shielded his eyes with a forearm, but the force of the wind still drove the grit against him like needles.

"Boone—wait!" Sadie cried, stumbling after him.

"He's not gonna stop," Jesse said.

"Jesse, we have to go with him!"

"We can't, Sadie!"

"We have no choice. We can't let him go alone!"

Scout barked, sharp and frantic, and tore after Boone.

Jesse and Sadie ran. The shoreline was unrecognizable. Waves smashed and collapsed sideways. Spray shot through the air in sheets that struck like cold needles. The only positive was that the current dragged everything inward from the ocean, toward Ocracoke. Boone was already knee-deep, gripping the john boat like it was the last solid thing in his world. Waves hammered his legs, nearly lifting him off balance with each surge. Fear flickered across his face, but determination forced its place beside it. His breath came out in ragged bursts, the storm ripping every exhale away before it fully left his lungs.

"LET'S GO!!!"

His voice ripped across the storm.

Jesse seized the canoe, bracing as the waves crashed into the shore. The cold water stung his legs.

The surge knocked him off balance, water climbing to his waist. The ocean didn't care if he was ready.

He steadied the hull for Sadie, who climbed in with trembling resolve. Scout leapt in beside her, crouched low, shivering but alert.

The dog's legs trembled against the hull, but she didn't whine, didn't cower. She faced the inlet like she'd faced every storm before—beside her people.

Sadie steadied herself with one hand on the gunwale, the other gripping the edge of her seat as the boat lurched under her weight.

She grabbed the paddle and dug it into the water before anyone told her to. No hesitation. They were doing this.

"We stay together — no matter what!" Jesse shouted.

A wave struck the canoe sideways, nearly wrenching it from his hands. He pushed harder. Sadie steadied herself. Boone fought the john boat forward. The storm roared around them, amplifying the thunder of their own hearts.

Wind in their face.

Water crashing into the hull.

The inlet heaved like a living thing, furious and unforgiving.

Behind them, the Life-Saving Station watched from the distance—the same building that had sheltered men who made this crossing a hundred years ago in the same conditions. Some of them had made it back. Some hadn't.

Together — shoulder to shoulder, hearts pounding, instincts screaming — they forced the boats deeper into the raging surf...

Toward Ocracoke.

Carried by the King Tide.

Boone's face had gone still—not calm, but committed. Whatever happened next, he wasn't turning back. None of them were.

Chapter Eleven

The Choice

The Carteret strained against the dock as if trying to tear itself free from the land. Every mooring line stretched, every inch of thick braided rope pulled tight. The tension hummed through the pilings. Each new gust carved across the Sound with enough force to shove the ferry sideways in its slip, the hull groaning under the push. The wheelhouse windows rattled continuously, glass quivering like it was being tested by a force that wanted to break it just to prove it could.

The storm pressed against the vessel with the insistence of something alive. The dock cleats, old cast iron worn down by decades of salt and strain, looked smaller than usual beneath the weight they held. Even the ferry's mast cables thrummed with a taut metallic whine, vibrating like bowstrings drawn too tight. Small flecks of peeling white paint lifted off the wheelhouse siding, torn free by the same wind that rocked the Carteret in sharp, erratic pulses.

Mist sprayed sideways, sweeping over the panes in jittery gray streaks that distorted the world beyond into a blurred, shifting watercolor of storm light. The horizon had dissolved into a smear of gray on gray. Nothing looked still. Nothing looked familiar. Everything looked like it was bracing.

Beyond the dock, the marsh grass bent nearly horizontal, battered into long, trembling lines that rippled like submerged hair. Loose sand scudded across the planks in thin, ghostlike trails. Gulls wheeled high overhead, their flight patterns jagged and uneasy, cries lost the moment they left their throats. Even the air carried a strange metallic sharpness, as though it had been scraped clean of all warmth and softness.

Beyond the dock, the Sound rolled with an unsettled chop—two- to four-foot swells rising and dropping in heavy, disorganized heaves. The sea surface began to tilt and fold in unnatural patterns, reorganizing itself under the influence of pressure the eye couldn't see but the water could not hide.

The water changed color too — shifting from its usual green-blue clarity into thicker, storm-dark layers of olive and slate. Patches of foam skittered across the surface, torn loose and flung aside like scraps. The current in the sound had taken on a jittery, unpredictable pulse, surging one way, then another, like a muscle flinching beneath a blow.

A storm was building its spine.

Inside the wheelhouse, another storm built its own.

Nautical charts lay folded beside the NOAA radio, edges softened by years of salt, sun, and bare-handed familiarity. A dull metal pencil rolled with every sway of the ferry, tapping the same knot in the wooden ledge with restless insistence. The NOAA radio crackled again—sharp bursts of static like electricity baring its teeth. It made the small room feel tighter, as though the weight of the storm was pressing inward through the walls.

Even the air inside had changed, thickening with humidity and unspent tension. The faint scent of old diesel and dried salt clung to the walls, familiar but somehow more aggressive in the confined space. A slow drip of condensation collected along the interior window frame, gathering weight until each droplet released and fell with a soft tap that echoed louder than it should have.

Caleb paced a narrow groove into the wheelhouse floor—one worn deeper by each minute he spent waiting. His uniform clung damply along the seams where sweat and salt air mixed. Shoulders squared too sharply.

Jaw clamped tight enough to ache. His gaze kept snapping to the radio... then to the keys hanging on their hook... then to his skiff tied to the auxiliary dock... then to Captain Riggs' empty chair.

Boots thudded against the metal floor, each step marked by a quick involuntary hitch of breath. The back of his neck prickled with sweat despite the chilly breeze sneaking through the window seams. His fingers flexed and curled at intervals, palms damp, as though fighting the instinct to grab something—anything—and act.

He didn't need the radio report. He knew the Sound's moods by instinct—by smell, by pressure, by the way the air tasted when a storm was gathering speed. He felt shifts in the wind like a man reading a language older than memory.

Still, he waited for the next NOAA update with the quiet desperation of someone hoping to be wrong.

Static sputtered, a voice broke through, thin and wavering.

"...Small Craft Advisory in effect through the afternoon. Winds fifteen to twenty-five knots. Seas two to four feet..."

Caleb stopped mid-step.

His hands balled into fists, knuckles whitening as the broadcast continued with merciless clarity.

"Conditions deteriorating through the afternoon, before subsiding tonight. Winds increasing to 20-25 knots with higher gusts... seas building 3-5 feet in Pamlico Sound..."

Each number landed like a punch.

Caleb's hand found the edge of the console and gripped it until his knuckles went white.

The shift from rough to dangerous.

From control to uncertainty.

A shift that echoed the one that had taken the lives of those tourists last year this time.

The air inside the wheelhouse seemed to shrink. The windows breathed inward with each gust, vibrating in their frames. Caleb's breath hitched once—small, barely perceptible—but enough to tighten the muscles along his ribs.

A gust slammed against the wheelhouse again, rattling the metal frame hard enough to buzz through the soles of his boots. Rain spattered in bursts, each drop sharp as a pinprick. Outside, in the distance, the inlet darkened to a deeper, heavier green, folds rising into thicker ridges. Caleb watched the water through the trembling glass, and something tugged hard inside him. A sensation he recognized far too well — the instinctive warning that came before every storm worth fearing.

A pressure coiled in his chest. Not panic. Not quite. But a knowing that lived deeper than fear—closer to memory.

The wheelhouse door banged open, slamming hard against the bulkhead. A blast of wind tore inside, flinging cold droplets across the floor. Captain Riggs stepped in, braced himself with boots planted wide. Even in this weather, he carried the quiet authority of a man who had battled storms big enough to have names.

Nearing retirement, weathered but steady, Riggs radiated the sort of grounded confidence born only from a lifetime working water that respected no one.

He paused in the doorway, studying Caleb.

"You're wearin' a groove in my deck, Caleb."

Caleb didn't smile. Didn't bother pretending. He kept staring at the inlet, where the water rose and folded in patterns only seasoned watermen would recognize as warnings.

"Cap... I need off for a bit. Couple hours."

Riggs set his clipboard down slowly, deliberately.

"You're on duty."

"We ain't runnin'," Caleb said. "Ferry's tied up. Schedule's shut down."

"Schedule's shut down," Riggs agreed, "Responsibility ain't."

Caleb's eyes flicked again to the hook where the keys hung—gleaming under the dim lights like an invitation. To the skiff tied at the auxiliary dock, his boat pitching and dipping on its lines.

His throat tightened.

"Those three tourists I was talkin' to yesterday mornin'—they were headed to Portsmouth. They... they weren't listenin'."

The girl had smiled at him. The wiry one had asked good questions. The third one—the tall one with the chip on his shoulder—had looked at him like he was the enemy.

His voice thinned. "I'm afraid they're gonna try comin' back in this. I should've—"

Words jammed in his chest, thick and hot.

Riggs softened only slightly. A man who had seen this look before.

"Storm like this... reminds me of the one last year that took the lives of those tourists."

Caleb didn't flinch outwardly, but the memory hit him like a cold spike driven straight through the ribs. He saw flashes — rain that blurred the world to nothing, wind screaming like something alive, a voice he couldn't reach in time. The moment the Sound swallowed what no rescue could undo.

He still heard it sometimes—the way a scream sounds when the water takes it. Half-voice, half-nothing.

"You were pacing just like this then, too," Riggs said, quieter now.

Caleb looked down, breath tightening. Sadie's face flickered through his mind—not the softness of admiration but the quiet trust she'd offered him. A trust he didn't feel he deserved, but couldn't bear to betray.

He'd given her his number. Told her to call if the weather turned. Had she kept it? Would she use it? Or had she already forgotten the local boy who'd warned her about the wind?

"Let me off, Cap," Caleb said, voice roughening. "I'm askin' ya, straight."

Riggs studied him with the kind of knowledge only years of watching a man work the water could give.

"You think I don't see when you're carryin' somethin' heavy, son?"

Caleb's throat worked around a swallow.

Rain struck the windows harder, a long, rolling sweep of Sound water flung sideways by a gust that made the entire ferry shudder.

Riggs nodded toward the storm-dark inlet.

"The ferry may need to run an emergency trip. I need my crew ready."

"I could take the skiff," Caleb said, too fast. "Be quick—"

"Before the tide swings?" Riggs cut in. "Before the inlet starts stackin' up?"

"The Sound don't care how good your intentions are, son."

A violent gust brushed the ferry broadside. The wheelhouse trembled. Riggs didn't move.

It was the kind of steady that comes only from surviving the worst storms without pretending they were anything less than monsters.

He shook his head once, final.

"Ain't gonna happen, Caleb. Not today."

Caleb took a step forward—barely, but enough to send a sharp tension through the air. His hands curled at his sides, jaw flexing. The memory of last fall pressed harder, suffocating.

Riggs didn't soften.

"Caleb... don't even think about it. Not on my watch. Those tourists ain't dumb enough to try to cross the inlet in this."

Caleb's eyes drifted to the keys again. He had to know for sure.

His hand lifted.

Inches from ending everything he'd worked to build.

The clean slate.

The trust Riggs had given him.

Then a memory returned — the glassy, mocking stillness of the Sound the morning after the storm last fall. The silence that had felt like punishment. The names he still carried like stones.

His hand curled slowly into a fist.

He lowered it.

His whole arm trembled with the effort.

"...Yes, sir."

The words dragged out of him like broken shells.

Caleb stepped to the side window and shoved it open. Wind punched through immediately, carrying the cold sting of rain and raw brine. Spray flecked across his face. Outside, in the distance, the inlet rolled harder — waves rising in jagged folds, water darkening into something with weight, something with intent.

He stared into the storm.

And the deeper storm inside him.

His hand twitched toward the keys again — a reflex he barely caught — and he forced it down with visible effort.

He didn't want another tragedy.

Not another name etched into his nights.

Not another choice made too late.

But the wind howled louder.

The ferry shuddered deeper.

The Sound darkened further.

This storm...

This storm felt like it was already deciding for him.

Somewhere out there, past the spray and the chop, three people were making a choice he couldn't stop.

Chapter Twelve

The Tide Turns

Late afternoon pressed a gray, bruised sky low over Ocracoke Inlet. The clouds churned like hammered steel—layers folding over one another, as though the sky were grinding down under its own weight. Far off, the horizon had disappeared behind a dark, trembling haze. Wind carved across the water in jagged, uneven sweeps, shifting direction every few seconds. Whitecaps ripped loose from the chop, flung sideways into mist that vanished almost as soon as it formed.

The tide slapped the aluminum and fiberglass hulls with hollow, discordant thuds—an unstable rhythm that warned of a shift beneath the surface. The inlet was turning, growing stranger by the minute, its behavior slipping further from predictability into something untamed. Something old. Something dangerous.

A thin, trembling sandbar of chop rose just above the tide line—the only scrap of refuge in an inlet that had abandoned safety entirely. Even that shallow patch shifted beneath them, trembling with each pulse of the current. Both the canoe and the johnboat rocked violently in the shallow water, held in place only by the desperate hands of the young men standing waist-deep beside them.

Boone and Jesse dug their feet into the unsteady ground, feeling the bar dissolve beneath them with each shift of the waves. Their toes searched for traction; their heels slipped deeper into the soft, sweeping pull of the sand. The current tugged at their legs in unpredictable bursts—sideways, forward, then eerily still, then suddenly surging as though something massive had turned beneath the inlet's surface.

Salty spray stung their eyes. The wind knifed across exposed skin, turning their fingers rigid and unresponsive. Each attempt to adjust their stance was answered with a fresh pulse of movement underfoot—sand liquefying, reshaping, betraying them. Boone glanced down every few seconds. The sandbar sank lower with each passing moment, narrowing beneath them.

Every few seconds, the sand shifted enough that both young men lost their balance and had to recover quickly. Boone's boots carved trenches into the bar that vanished almost instantly. Jesse felt grains sliding around his ankles, a silent, sucking pull drawing him off the bar entirely. His calves burned with the fight to stay upright, muscles trembling from constant correction.

The air itself seemed to thicken with unease, carrying the heavy salt of stormwater that had traveled a long distance. Beneath all the noise—the shriek of wind, the slosh and slap of water—there was a deeper undertone, a subcurrent sound like a low, rolling growl within the inlet. Jesse wasn't sure if it was the tide or his imagination, but it made the hair on his arms rise.

In the canoe, Sadie crouched low with Scout pressed tight against her chest. The dog's trembling worsened, her entire body quivering in frantic pulses. Scout's ribs heaved against Sadie's arms as she struggled to breathe. Each of her breaths came uneven—short, panicked gasps cut by blasts of wind. Her ears pinned flat every time the gale shrieked overhead, and her claws dug involuntarily into Sadie's jacket.

Sadie pressed her cheek against the top of Scout's head for a heartbeat, drawing in the faint warmth rising from her fur. The gesture steadied her just enough to keep her from shaking apart. Her lungs felt too tight, as though the storm had crept inside and made a home between her ribs.

The canoe rocked again, harder this time, forcing her to shift her weight to stay upright. Beneath her, the hull vibrated with every slap of the waves.

"This is bad, Boone! Look at that water up ahead!" Jesse shouted.

Boone and Jesse turned toward the deeper channel. The water ahead had gone nearly black, threaded with diagonal currents slicing into one another like crossed blades. Nothing flowed in any recognizable direction. The surface twisted and spiraled, alive in a way no water should be. Even from this distance, the channel looked hostile—throbbing, waiting.

A gust hit them broadside, forcing Boone to brace his entire forearm against the johnboat's gunwale. The hull slammed repeatedly into his hip, each impact radiating through bone.

Boone forced confidence into his voice, though his grip tightened on the johnboat.

"We've come this far. The King Tide has helped us get to this point. We're over half way."

But the tension in his shoulders betrayed him. He swallowed hard, jaw muscles twitching beneath wind-chapped skin.

Sadie leaned forward, fear sharpening her voice. Her breath came out in sharp bursts, barely audible under the roar.

"We've still got the worst part ahead!"

Her knuckles whitened around the gunwales as a gust slammed them sideways. The canoe shuddered violently, making the wooden thwarts creak in protest.

"We won't make it across that next channel! It's too rough!" Jesse yelled.

Scout barked sharply—fearfully—before the wind ripped the sound away.

Sadie's instincts snapped into focus. Every fiber of her body screamed for action, for something—anything—that might shift the odds in their favor.

"We need to call someone. Jesse, do you have service?"

Jesse fumbled open his dry bag, fingers stiff with cold. He pulled out his phone—its black screen slick with saltwater.

Nothing.

Black screen.

Dead.

"Damn—it's dead. Soaked."

"We're not calling anyone!" Boone snapped.

"Why? You worried how you'll look?" Jesse fired back.

Boone's jaw tightened. Pride, fear, and something deeper twisted through his expression.

"Worried we've already wasted too much time standing here!"

Waves slammed the canoe, soaking Sadie's face. She twisted shoulder-first into the blast, shielding Scout as cold dug deeper into her bones. The dog whimpered and tucked closer, burying her snout against Sadie's chest.

"Boone... I was counting on you to get us back safe. That's not what this is."

Her voice wavered, but her gaze held steady.

"I'm not asking you to be a hero, Boone. I'm asking you to hear us."

Boone didn't answer. His eyes stayed locked on the churning water ahead—the place where he wanted control to still exist, even as it slipped away. His breathing had gone shallow.

Jesse's frustration broke free.

"We need help."

Sadie closed her eyes for half a second—just long enough for desperation to surface. She pulled a damp, crumpled scrap of paper from her pocket—the ink slightly blurred.

Caleb's number.

She had committed it to memory the night before, by the fire.

Jesse stiffened. His heartbeat surged.

"What's that?"

"It's Caleb's number."

"You think he'd come?"

"I don't know... I think he would."

The wind tried to rip the paper from her fingers. Sadie curled her palm around it protectively. Boone jerked back as if the name itself wounded him.

"You're not seriously thinking of calling him, are you?"

"He's the only one we know on the island," Sadie said.

The current surged beneath them—another reminder that they were running out of choices. Boone's shoulders tightened. Fear and jealousy warred visibly across his face, hitting him harder than the inlet's currents.

Sadie pulled out her phone. Her fingers shook violently—part cold, part pure terror.

"I think we should call Caleb."

"No way!" Boone shouted, spinning toward her so fast the johnboat rocked again.

"He knows these waters. He'd come for us. I know he would."

"Absolutely not. No way in hell."

Scout whimpered at the sharpness in Boone's voice, shrinking deeper against Sadie.

"He's a ferry hand, Boone," Jesse said. "Not the devil."

And that was when Boone cracked.

"He's a snake and you know it. You've seen the way he looks at her. And the way she looks back."

Lightning could not have cut through them sharper.

Sadie froze, breath stolen clean from her lungs. Hurt washed across her face in a way that made Jesse's stomach turn. Even the wind seemed to drop for a beat.

Jesse stepped in front of her instinctively, shoulders squared between them.

His heart hammered against his ribs. This wasn't how it was supposed to go. Not the trip, not the storm, not any of it.

"This isn't about pride, or jealousy, or some high school drama. This is about not dying in this inlet."

"You're not seeing what this water's doing to us. Open your eyes, man."

Boone's voice splintered, anger collapsing inward into something more frightened, more fragile.

"You call him if you want. I'll go ahead on my own."

She didn't want to need him. Didn't want to prove Boone right about anything. But pride was a luxury for people who weren't about to drown.

Sadie dialed with shaking hands. The phone felt slippery, unreliable.

For a moment, the phone lit up. A faint ring bled through static.

"Caleb? We're in the inlet—please—"

A wave slammed the canoe. Cold water crashed across her chest and shoulders. She twisted her body, shielding the phone.

The screen flickered.

Glitched.

Died.

"No... no, no—"

"What is it?" Jesse shouted.

"It's dead. The water... the spray... I think it fried it."

Boone watched, expression unreadable.

"Guess he ain't coming after all."

Sadie stared at the dead screen. She'd done everything right. The island had told her to hold onto that number. And it hadn't been enough.

Sadie's voice cracked.

"Boone... please. If you don't want to call Caleb—then call 911. Call the Coast Guard."

"Seriously, man," Jesse added. "Call somebody. We're out of options."

Boone stared at them, denial layered so thick it had become armor.

"There's no signal out here. It won't work. We're wasting time."

It was a lie.

He knew it.

But admitting he was wrong felt harder than drowning.

"Boone—"

"NO!" he barked.

"No more standing around! We push to the next sandbar. Let's GO."

He yanked the johnboat outward into the chop. The current grabbed hold instantly, pulling it sideways with violent intent. Boone wrestled it, muscles straining, water swirling higher around his waist. His breaths came ragged now.

Scout whimpered and clawed frantically at Sadie's soaked jacket.

Sadie and Jesse exchanged a look—fear, determination, and resignation all wound tight.

Then they pushed off.

Together. The way they'd done everything since they were kids. The way they'd finish this—one way or another.

The inlet reacted immediately.

The canoe jerked away from the sandbar, almost ripped from Jesse's grip. Sadie lurched, planting a knee to steady herself. The hull shook violently under them.

Wind sliced across the water, cold and sharp, finding every gap in their clothing. Spray thickened into a stinging mist that clung to their faces. Their breath fogged in white bursts. Scout's fur plastered flat against her, her trembling returning in sharp waves.

The tide beneath them deepened into a heavier pull. It felt less like water and more like a massive throat drawing inward.

"The current is starting to pull us out!" Jesse yelled, fighting to angle the bow.

"We're not going toward Ocracoke anymore!" Sadie cried.

"We're heading toward the ocean!"

Ahead—where the inlet met the Atlantic—a massive breaker rose on the bar.

A white, towering wall.

A living cliff.

A force with no mercy.

The sound reached them first—a deep, hollow thunder that vibrated through the hull and into their bones.

"We have to turn back!" Sadie screamed.

"We can't turn in this!" Boone yelled.

"If we get sucked into those breakers we're done!" Jesse shouted.

A rising swell caught the canoe sharply, lifting it to a dizzying angle. Spray lashed across them. Scout howled, scrambling for any grip as the boat pitched beneath her. Her claws clattered uselessly against the slick fiberglass floor.

Then Scout stopped scrambling. She pressed flat against Sadie's legs and went still—bracing for what was coming.

"Paddle! Left—turn us left!" Jesse shouted.

They fought—arms burning, lungs screaming, muscles failing against the inlet's power. Paddles tore through water that resisted every stroke. The storm swallowed every sound except effort and fear.

Boone rowed straight toward the chaos.

"Boone! Stop!" Sadie cried.

"I've got it! I can push through!" he yelled.

The breaker rose higher.

Closer.

Closer—a towering white monster swallowing the sky.

The roar drowned everything.

And then—

IMPACT.

Chapter Thirteen

Wind, Water, Darkness

The inlet had become a living thing—an enraged, shifting creature made of wind, water, and violent sound. It breathed in long, dragging pulls and exhaled in explosive sheets of spray that tore across the shrinking afternoon like shrapnel. What little daylight remained thinned into a bruised haze, the sky folding inward as though the storm were swallowing sun, color, and distance all at once.

The air itself felt pulled across invisible teeth, each gust shredding the edges of sound before the next came to erase whatever remained.

Waves rose like walls—steep, vertical, sudden—and crashed into the johnboat and canoe with crushing force. Every impact shook their bones. Every one pushed the line between staying upright and disappearing beneath the storm. White water detonated across both bows, the spray hitting their skin so sharply it felt like slicing blades. Foam cascaded over the gunwales again and again, heavy and cold, filling every crevice until it seemed the boats themselves were melting into the storm's rage.

The constant hammering had rhythm—if chaos could be said to have rhythm—like a drumbeat played by something ancient and furious. Each slam into the hull vibrated through their knees, their spines, their teeth.

Spray knifed sideways, stinging their faces, blinding their eyes. The air tasted of salt and grit—like breathing broken seashells. The wind screamed with a voice that could have belonged to a living, furious thing: high-pitched one moment, guttural the next.

It sounded almost sentient—almost aware of them—finding new ways to strike, new angles to claw at skin and bone.

The water had lost all color. No blues, no greens—only slate gray, white, and pitch-black voids between towering crests. The inlet had become a funnel, its current thick as rope, dragging them toward the mouth where the open Atlantic waited like a predator. Every pull of the tide felt heavier than the last, as if unseen hands beneath the surface were gripping the canoe and johnboat.

In the canoe, Scout pushed tight against Sadie's legs. Scout's entire body shook—rapid, relentless pulses that trembled through Sadie's shins. Her breath came in short, panicked bursts between shrieks of wind. Her ears lay pinned flat, and her claws dug into the deck with desperate instinct.

She could feel every tremor in Scout, each one syncing with the rising dread in her own stomach.

"Y'all hang on!" Jesse shouted, though the wind shredded the words almost before they left his mouth.

They broke apart and scattered instantly, swallowed by the shrieking storm.

"Scout! Hold on, baby — hold on!" Sadie cried, coughing as spray hit her throat and mouth, flooding her gasp with cold.

Salt stung the back of her tongue. She coughed again, eyes burning.

A massive wave smashed over them. The canoe groaned under the impact, the hull flexing like something near its breaking point. For a heartbeat, they were submerged—darkness, weight, cold—and they broke back into the world, leaning hard left and right to counterbalance, Scout scrambling helplessly.

Sadie's hair slapped across her face, soaked, plastered to her cheeks. Jesse blinked rapidly, forcing burning seawater from his eyes.

And then—

Boone's johnboat flipped.

There was no warning.

No slow roll.

No chance to brace.

The wave hit it like a giant hand had seized the stern and hurled it skyward. One moment Boone was upright, fighting the bow into the swell, and the next he was airborne—weightless—then slammed into angry water like a stone dropped from a cliff.

His breath vanished in a burst of bubbles.

His mind blanked.

His body folded into the cold.

Sound vanished into muffled roar.

Light fractured.

Cold swallowed him whole.

The current seized him instantly, turning him sideways, rolling him, dragging him. Up became down. Down became sideways. Sideways became nothing familiar. Saltwater forced itself into his nose and mouth. His lungs burned with the sting. His arms pinwheeled as he fought for orientation, any point of stability—sand, hull, even pain—anything that wasn't this freefall through liquid darkness.

His foot hit sand—then slid—then brushed it again.

A shoal.

Shallow—barely—but enough.

Boone surged upward, breaking the surface in a violent gasp. He coughed hard, choking between waves that struck his head like fists. His limbs felt slow, numb, as if wrapped in ice. He clawed for breath, for direction, for anything stable.

The johnboat's overturned hull smashed into him, bruising his ribs. The bowline whipped across his waist.

The blow shocked him, snapped through the haze, pulled him back into himself.

Instinct took over.

Not logic.

Not fear.

Pure survival.

Boone tore at his rain jacket with trembling hands, fingers barely responding, fighting the cold. He yanked out the zip-lock bag he'd checked religiously all day. Inside—his phone. His only lifeline.

The bag was slick, his hands shaking so badly that it slipped once—twice—nearly vanishing into the churn.

He nearly dropped it.

Caught it.

Fumbled.

Almost lost it again.

Caught it once more.

The world pitched violently around him.

His heart hammered.

His vision flickered with panic.

All that pride. All that refusal. And now he was begging a stranger to save them because he hadn't listened when it mattered.

He pressed 9-1-1.

The wind shoved him sideways.

Ringing.

Ringing.

Ringing—

The call connected.

"911, what's your emergency?"

"We're in Ocracoke Inlet! The current — it's pulling us out! Boats capsized! We're in the water!"

His voice cracked, swallowed between sobs. Another wave struck his back, shoving him forward in a violent lurch.

"Sir, try to stay calm. What is your exact location?"

He was coughing, throat raw.

"Please... please... save us... please..."

His voice broke into the wind, shredded into thin pieces.

"I am contacting the Coast Guard and National Park Service now. Stay on the line. Do you see any land or lights?"

He spun in the water, searching.

Nothing.

No shore.

No dunes.

No sky—just blackening cloud and rising walls of water.

"I can't— I can't see—anything—"

"Sir, hold on. Do NOT hang up—"

The phone buzzed.

Flickered.

Died.

Boone stared at the black screen as though the universe itself had betrayed him. A sound tore out of him—raw, feral, broken. The storm ripped it away.

He'd swallowed his pride. He'd asked for help. And the universe had hung up on him anyway.

The canoe drifted farther from him with every surge. Swamped, barely afloat. Jesse and Sadie clung to the slippery gunnels, their bodies shaking violently from exertion and cold. Scout howled in terror, her paws sliding helplessly on the fiberglass.

The howl rose, broke and rose again, cutting through the wind with a desperate sharpness that made Sadie's heart twist.

She'd brought Scout here. Into this. If the dog didn't make it, that was on Sadie.

Sadie wrapped one arm around the dog, the other grasping the gunnel.

Her fingers were stiff, cramping, nearly numb.

Jesse gripped both sides, his muscles screaming from strain. Paddling was futile now. His forearms trembled uncontrollably. His teeth chattered between clenched breaths.

"Boone!!" Sadie screamed, her voice ripped into nothing.

"I can't see Boone!" Jesse yelled, even though she could not hear him.

A faint pulse of red flickered through the gray chaos.

Sadie blinked hard.

Again.

Again—

The buoy.

The blinking channel marker.

Their last point before the Atlantic.

"Oh God... we're past it," Jesse said, voice cracking.

The marker shrank behind them, swallowed by storm and distance.

Past that buoy, there was nothing. No sandbars. No shelter. Just open ocean and whatever the Atlantic decided to do with them.

"Jesse — the current — we can't paddle against it — the canoe is sunk!"

Another wave slammed into them. The canoe dipped dangerously, nearly rolling over. Scout shrieked in fear.

They had lost control.

The inlet had taken it.

Boone clung to the johnboat's overturned hull, breath jagged, waves smashing him repeatedly. His fingers were numb, his arms barely responding.

He screamed again—

"No, no, no...!"

His voice vanished.

Sadie, Jesse, and Scout drifted through towering, black mountains of water. Each new rise threatened to peel their fingers free. Their muscles burned. Their lungs stung.

Through shifting walls of water, they glimpsed Boone again—

A silhouette.

A flailing arm.

A flash of motion.

Then—

Gone.

The inlet swallowed him.

"We're losing Boone," Jesse said, his voice cracking.

Everything he'd wanted to say. Everything he'd held back for twelve years. None of it mattered now if they didn't survive the next ten minutes.

His throat tightened.

"Sadie, stay with me. If we panic, we're done."

Sadie's breath trembled. Pain radiated through her muscles, cold settling deep into her bones. Scout pressed into her for warmth, terror shaking her violently. She tucked her chin low, trying to shield the dog from the worst of the spray, though it felt like shielding a candle from a hurricane.

The island had promised something. She'd felt it. But now the island was silent, and the ocean was taking them anyway.

Thunder rolled overhead—deep, ancient—a warning from something older than storms.

The island had been watching all along. Now it was speaking.

The sound vibrated through the water, through the canoe, through their ribs.

The sky collapsed into black.

The water rose higher.

The wind sharpened until it screamed.

"Jesse... what if help doesn't come?" Sadie whispered through chattering teeth.

Jesse's eyes met hers—fear finally visible.

But beneath it—stubborn resolve.

"We hold on 'til it does."

He tightened his grip on the hull until his knuckles went white.

Daylight drained away—gray to charcoal, charcoal to black.

The storm roared louder, swallowing the world around them until only three things remained:

Wind.

Water.

And the relentless voice of a storm that had decided to break the inlet open.

Chapter Fourteen

Done Waiting

Dusk pressed itself against the Carteret — thick, merciless, and strangely intent — wrapping the ferry in a storm that felt alive and watching. The dark had weight, the kind that pressed down with a slow, deliberate hand, as though the sky itself were leaning into the Sound and trying to smother everything beneath it. Wind and rain pelted the pilot house in violent, uneven bursts, each gust landing differently, as though the gale were learning the ferry's defenses, testing her weak points, choosing where to strike next. Some gusts were glancing, sharp slaps across the metal; others were deep, resonant blows that made the entire vessel tremble as though something enormous had rammed her broadside.

Rain sheeted sideways, driven so hard it behaved more like spray torn from breaking seas than anything falling from clouds. It struck the wheelhouse glass in relentless, blurred smears of colorless light, streaking downward before being ripped away again by the wind. Beyond the windows the horizon was fading — no sky, no waterline, no separation between sound and storm. Only a heaving, surging dark that swallowed every reference point. Blurred shapes in the distance dissolved before they could form. Even the familiar outline of the dock bled into shadow, consumed by the storm's growing appetite.

Even tied securely to the dock, the ferry shifted restlessly, as if she too felt the storm's pressure and wanted to flee. Thick mooring lines stretched until they hummed, eased, then stretched again, each cycle punctuated by heavy, gut-deep thunks as the cleats absorbed the strain. Every vibration traveled through the pilot house floor, rising through boots and bones alike. It was a storm that weighed on a man's lungs. A storm that pushed against the ribs. A storm seasoned watermen recognized instantly — the moment before bad becomes dangerous, and dangerous becomes something else entirely. It was the kind of night that took stories out of a man's past and replayed them in his head whether he wanted them or not.

Inside, muted red night-lights bathed the wheelhouse in a low, war-room glow. Shadows moved like slow creatures across the bulkheads and chart table, shifting with every sway of the ferry. The NOAA weather report murmured overhead, the calm monotone feeling almost cruel in its indifference to the violence outside. The VHF hissed and crackled with sharp bursts of static, each one snagging nerves already pulled tight. Every now and then, a burst of interference thumped through the speakers like a heartbeat.

Caleb paced.

Back and forth.

Back and forth.

Boots landing in the same scuffed path he'd worn into the steel deck. His pacing had a rhythm to it — sharp turns at either end, a slight press of his palm against the bulkhead. Every few steps, he stopped at the forward windows, leaning so close his breath fogged the glass. He squinted into the storm, as if sheer focus might force the inlet to reveal its secrets. But nothing presented itself — only shifting layers of rain and blackness sucking up whatever light existed.

Water streaked along the pane in serpentine lines, catching the red glow and twisting it into broken shapes. Sometimes, in the distorted glass, Caleb saw himself as he felt: stretched thin, pulled tight as the mooring lines outside.

A cold, instinctive truth tightened in his chest.

Not a thought.

Not a fear.

A knowing that those three — might be out there.

The girl with the smile. The one who'd talked to him at Dajio like he was worth knowing. She'd kept his number — he'd seen her tuck it into her pocket.

He pressed his fingertips against the window's edge, feeling the vibration of the wind through the steel frame. His nails tapped once, twice — a tiny, anxious rhythm he didn't consciously intend. Outside, the dock lights flickered beneath sheets of rain, briefly revealing the ghostly blur of foam sweeping across the pilings. In that momentary illumination, the storm didn't look random. It looked intentional.

Another violent burst of wind crashed against the wheelhouse, rattling metal framing and making loose tools clatter. A stack of papers fluttered and settled. The lights flickered once, recovering with a low electrical hum. Caleb's eyes flashed toward the keys hanging on the bulkhead — brass glinting in the red glow — toward the window, back to the keys.

His jaw tightened.

His breath deepened.

Something in him shifted — quietly, but unmistakably.

Captain Riggs sat in the helm chair, a chart open before him. He wasn't reading it. His eyes lifted every few seconds, studying Caleb with a look that held equal parts sympathy and worry. Riggs had been through too many storms not to recognize the one building inside the young man pacing his wheelhouse. He could see the tightening of shoulders, the restless hands, the way Caleb's boots struck the deck a little harder each time he turned.

Riggs exhaled through his nose, a slow, deliberate breath, trying to steady the air between them. He rubbed his knuckles absently, as though recalling storms he'd tried — and sometimes failed — to outthink when he was Caleb's age. He knew the look of a man about to break an order, or make one.

Then it came.

The VHF BLARED — a sharp, piercing alarm that cut clean through the storm's roar.

Caleb froze mid-stride.

"PON-PON, PON-PON, PON-PON. All stations, all stations, all stations — this is United States Coast Guard Sector North Carolina..."

Caleb's breath abandoned him.

His stomach dropped.

His blood turned electric.

"Report of multiple small craft swamped or overturned in the vicinity of Ocracoke Inlet. All mariners advised—"

Riggs looked up sharply, tension snapping across his tired features. His hand hovered above the chart, no longer pretending to read it.

"Might not be them," he said.

But Caleb had already gone pale.

"It's them," he whispered.

The VHF continued, signal struggling under heavy interference:

"Conditions deteriorating... vessels may be drifting seaward... keep sharp lookout—"

Before the transmission could finish, the wheelhouse door blasted open, slamming so hard it nearly rebounded off the bulkhead. A violent gust shoved rain into the room in a horizontal burst. Cold droplets peppered the floor, the chart, Caleb's sleeves. A Park Service officer stepped in, soaked from hat to boots, water streaming off him in rivulets. Behind him hovered the Mate — pale, shaken, drenched. Their presence alone confirmed the severity; Park Service didn't appear on the ferry unless something serious broke loose.

"Captain Riggs — Coast Guard just called. Multiple individuals. At least one small craft overturned in the inlet."

Caleb's chest tightened until something inside him buckled.

He knew.

He had known from the first syllable.

"It's those kids... " Riggs whispered.

Caleb lunged for his slicker. His hands shook as he shoved his arms into the sleeves, the fabric slapping wildly in the wind. His fingers fumbled with the zipper, cold rainwater making the metal slippery.

"Caleb —" Riggs warned, rising to his feet.

"I'm done waiting."

Caleb crossed the wheelhouse in three long, decisive strides. He snatched the keys off the hook with a metallic scrape, turned toward the open doorway, shoulders squared like a man walking straight into gunfire.

"Caleb — wait."

The word cut through everything.

Caleb stopped. Riggs stepped in front of him, not blocking his path entirely, but halting him with purpose. Rain hammered the doorway behind him, cold spray whipping inside.

In his hand was a heavy, old handheld VHF — the emergency unit that had outlived storms, captains, and decades. Its casing was scratched, the antenna wrapped in tape, the speaker grill dented from some forgotten night. Riggs held it out like a man offering a weapon to someone walking into battle.

"Take this."

Caleb hesitated, then reached out and took it. His fingers curled tightly around the radio.

He wasn't going alone. Riggs would be listening and passing info to the Coast Guard.

"Keep us updated on 16," Riggs said. "I'll relay to the Coast Guard."

Riggs gripped Caleb's shoulder, just for a second. "Make sure you come back, son. You hear me?"

"Thank you, Captain."

He bolted into the night.

Riggs moved to the doorway, watching him sprint down the long pier, swallowed by sheets of rain within seconds. The storm hammered the ferry again, and Riggs' face folded in quiet dread.

The pier lights flickered as Caleb ran. Rain struck him like thrown gravel. Wind shoved him sideways with every step. He steadied himself on a piling, breath tearing from his lungs, jacket whipping wildly around him. The handheld radio dug into his palm. The keys rattled like loose bones in his fist.

The docks moaned beneath the force of the wind, wooden planks flexing and protesting with each gust. Ropes slapped against masts, metal rings clanged against pilings, and every sound felt sharpened by urgency.

His skiff fought the dock like a live thing. The bow snatched with each gust, pressing against the fenders and straining the lines. Spray blasted across its deck, washing through the scuppers. The boat looked wild, angry — ready to leap headlong into the storm.

Caleb reached her, tossed the stern line free, and the bow. Both disappeared instantly into the dark. The boat swung broadside, wind nearly knocking him backwards across the slick planks. His boots skidded, catching just enough grip to keep him upright.

He braced.

Jumped aboard.

Caught the rail as his boots slid.

Cold rain washed across his face. His breath caught from the shock.

He jammed the key into the ignition. The outboard coughed, sputtered.

For one terrible second, he thought the storm had already won.

Then it roared awake, vibrating through the hull in a deep, aggressive growl.

Caleb backed her cleanly away from the dock, instinct guiding motions his mind barely registered. He spun her into the wind — the bow rising and slapping hard — then gunned the throttle.

The storm hit him full in the face.

The Sound was asking him the same question it had asked a hundred years of watermen before him: Are you sure?

Wind clawed at him with open hands.

Rain struck like needles.

Waves rose without warning, slamming the bow upward before dropping the skiff into troughs deep enough to erase the world.

Spray exploded over him, drenching him instantly through every layer. The cold shot straight into his bones.

He flattened himself into the console, gripped the wheel with one hand and the radio with the other, breath sharp and trembling.

Darkness swallowed the shoreline behind him.

Ahead — only a narrow spear of bow-light cutting into a world of black water and rising walls.

And still, he pushed forward.

He did not hesitate.

He did not look back.

Last year's faces flickered through him—the ones he hadn't reached in time. He wasn't going to add three more.

He whispered into the storm's teeth:

"Hold on, Sadie... just hold on..."

A towering swell lifted the bow, held it suspended like a judgment, then slammed the skiff down in a bone-rattling crash. Spray burst around him like shattered glass.

Caleb tightened his grip and drove deeper into the violent night —

Into the Sound,

Into the storm,

Into the place where the inlet was breaking open.

Somewhere ahead, three people were fighting to survive. He was done watching from the dock.

He did not slow down.

Chapter Fifteen

Heros

The MH-65 USCG Helicopter Dolphin surged north along the storm-distorted coastline, its bright orange fuselage glowing faintly each time lightning shattered the sky into fractured white veins. Each flash made the aircraft appear almost suspended in midair, frozen for an instant before plunging again into the heaving dark. The helicopter bucked and reeled in the wind, rotors slicing through chaotic gusts that clawed at the frame with feral force. Metal groaned under the strain, a deep, flexing vibration that made even seasoned crew members tighten their grips.

Inside, heat radiated from the turbines, mixing with the cold bite of rainwater sucked into the vents. The air itself felt conflicted—hot at their backs, icy on their faces. Every vibration traveled up their spines, rattling through bone and teeth. The cabin hummed with the hard, metallic pulse of a machine fighting weather that did not want to be fought. Even through their headsets, the world felt loud and intimate, as if the storm had crawled inside the aircraft with them.

The crew knew this kind of night.

This kind of storm.

This exact flavor of dread and duty.

Everyone in the cabin carried memories of the moment when nature decided whether to show mercy—or take something it would never return.

That silent accounting lived somewhere in their ribs, a quiet ledger no amount of training erased.

Petty Officer Lucas Hartley, the rescue swimmer, sat with one gloved hand hooked into the overhead bar, the other braced firmly on his knee as the aircraft jolted again. His visor reflected streaks of black and gray, ocean and storm layered in a blur beneath them. Occasional flashes of lightning carved sharp silhouettes across the water, but nothing stayed visible long enough to trust.

Rain hammered the fuselage like thrown gravel, distorting every beam of light the Dolphin cast downward. The sound was relentless, a metallic rattling that seeped into the cabin until it felt like part of the aircraft's heartbeat. Hartley's harness buzzed against his chest, rattling faintly each time turbulence twisted the air around them. He breathed through the motion, muscles flexing in small, controlled adjustments to stay steady.

He leaned closer to catch the copilot's voice through the comms.

"Sector, this is Three-Four-Five-Five. Commencing low-altitude sweep south of the inlet. Visibility a quarter mile, ceiling decreasing."

Static chewed at the edges of the transmission. The storm warped each syllable as though biting down on the signal, compressing it, tearing small pieces away.

"Copy, Three-Four-Five-Five. Maintain search pattern Delta. Wind, current and drift could have subjects farther outside the inlet by this point."

Hartley exhaled slowly, controlled, letting the breath settle the tightness in his chest.

Outside the Inlet.

In a storm like this?

Multiple people. That was all dispatch had. No names, no ages, no details. Just voices in the water before the line went dead.

An understanding slid deeper into him, steady and unwelcome. People didn't last long out here. Not in open water. Not in this violence. He knew the statistics, the brutal mathematics. Hypothermia. Impact trauma. Exhaustion. Disorientation. Panic. Each one a predator waiting its turn.

People thought drowning was peaceful—a quiet slipping away.

It wasn't. Not in weather like this.

He'd seen the truth up close: the body fighting beyond reason, then failing suddenly, shockingly fast. The ocean didn't negotiate. It simply decided.

Lightning split the sky again. For an instant, the roiling ocean lit up beneath them—whitecaps snarling like teeth. Waves no longer moved in recognizable sets; they collided from mixed directions, tall, broken, monstrous, their peaks shredded by wind before they could fully form. The surface looked less like water and more like a battlefield in motion.

The pilot steadied the aircraft with practiced shoulders and calm hands. His movements were slow and deliberate, countering the storm with the assured steadiness of someone who had lived too many nights like this.

"Alright," he said, voice low but firm. "Eyes out. Anything—colors, shapes, debris, life jackets."

The crew's posture shifted as one, shoulders leaning slightly toward the windows, breathing syncing with the rhythm of the search pattern. Hartley pressed his visor to the cold window. His breath fogged the inside before clearing again, leaving only the violent smear of black and white beneath him. The cold glass numbed the bridge of his nose, a sensation he welcomed—it gave him something fixed to anchor against.

He'd always believed he could sense when the ocean was hiding something—not literally, but storms like this carried a different kind of silence below the roar. A weight that sank into the ribs.

Tonight, the ocean felt like it was keeping a secret.

A cruel one.

Flight mechanic Morgan leaned forward, headset tight against his ears. He squinted into the shifting dark.

The Dolphin tilted with a shudder, dipping just enough for Hartley to get a clearer view. Spray blasted upward in ghostly, chaotic towers as the searchlight pierced down in a thin, trembling spear.

The beam skimmed the surface—water, spray, nothing.

Water, spray, nothing.

Hartley swallowed hard. The rhythm of searching without finding was its own kind of dread, a slow tightening of the chest that crept inward with each pass of the light.

Not finding debris could mean they missed the trail.

Or that the ocean had already pulled everything under.

The pilot spoke again, voice still steady but edged with strain.

"Coming up on the shoals. Watch the swell surge."

A gust rolled under the aircraft, yanking it downward in a sudden drop. Hartley's stomach jolted. Morgan grabbed the rail overhead, boots braced wide, the motion instinctive and practiced.

Still nothing.

Nothing but the chaotic churn of a storm that felt personal.

Lightning blazed—a fierce, jagged sheet—illuminating the storm wall and wind-driven rain sweeping horizontally across open water. The kind of rain that acted like sandpaper. The kind that peeled skin. The kind that made rescue operations a brutal negotiation between courage and physics.

Hartley knew that haze intimately.

He had been lowered into it once.

Only once.

The memory still tightened his throat, a phantom cold working its way down the back of his neck. His fingers flexed around the overhead bar, knuckles whitening.

Morgan's voice crackled through. "Swimmer, eyes up. Partial silhouette or we prep the cable."

Hartley nodded, though Morgan likely couldn't see it in the dim cabin light. His muscles stayed coiled, ready. His heart matched the rotor cadence—steady, heavy, insistent.

The Dolphin covered another half-mile.

Then another.

Rain.

Spray.

Darkness.

Sector's voice returned through worsening static:

"Three-Four-Five-Five, be advised... drift model update... search radius expanded southeast... surface conditions worsening... report turbulence severity."

The copilot replied:

"Severe. Gusting over twenty-five knots. Rain interference high."

A beat of silence.

Then:

"Copy. Continue until bingo fuel."

Hartley closed his eyes for two seconds.

Not a prayer—but close.

He'd pulled survivors from impossible conditions.

He'd held limp bodies in his arms.

He'd fought water colder than this.

He'd jumped into hell for people who never learned his name.

His daughter had asked him once why he did it. He still didn't have a good answer. Just that someone had to.

But he had learned one truth none of them spoke aloud:

Rescuers don't save people.

They just try to reach them before the ocean decides.

The searchlight swept again—

And there.

A flicker.

A shape.

Hartley leaned in, breath held.

"Pilot! Hold—hold—back it up—light on that!"

The Dolphin shifted, searchlight pinning the object floating low in the chop.

A cooler lid.

Only a cooler lid.

Hartley's jaw flexed. His shoulders tightened, then slowly eased.

The pilot said quietly, "Not helpful—but logged."

They pressed on.

The next gust slammed the aircraft hard—enough to tilt it sharply before the pilot recovered. Hartley gripped the overhead bar tight, boots sliding slightly across the wet deck. The metal beneath him vibrated violently, a reminder of how thin the line was between control and catastrophe.

Morgan swore under his breath.

"That's it. Swimmer stays in unless we get a live contact."

Hartley didn't argue.

A hoist in this weather was suicide.

Even with a live target, it would test everything they had. He felt the unspoken weight of that truth settle among the crew. No bravado tonight. Only skill, caution, and the storm's indifferent rules.

The copilot scanned again, jaw clenched, fatigue settling into his shoulders in small, almost imperceptible curves.

"Approaching inlet mouth," he said. His voice dropped. "Zero visibility past the shoals."

Beneath them, the storm inhaled—drawing water upward in violent columns. The inlet churned like a cauldron overturned, currents ripping in conflicting directions. Hartley had never seen it behave like this. He doubted many living had.

Morgan murmured, "If they made it this far... nobody swims through that."

Nobody.

The searchlight swept one final arc across the boiling inlet.

Nothing.

No color.

No movement.

No bright flash of life jackets.

No bodies.

Sector returned, voice distorted:

"Three-Four-Five-Five... approaching bingo fuel... recommend abort... return to base."

The pilot hesitated.

Looking down.

Jaw set.

Wanting two more minutes.

Somewhere down there, someone was still fighting. He could feel it.

Knowing two more minutes might cost the aircraft.

Morgan placed a hand on his shoulder.

It was the hardest thing a crew member ever had to do—tell someone to stop trying.

"It's over, sir."

A long beat.

"Sector, Three-Four-Five-Five. Aborting search due to fuel and conditions. Returning to base."

The words fell like weight in the cabin. No one shifted. No one breathed too loudly. The admission always felt the same—like closing a door you wished could stay open a little longer.

Hartley swallowed hard. He had been here before—too many times. Searching until the night itself decided the mission was finished. Leaving with the knowledge that the ocean still held its answers somewhere in the dark.

He shut his eyes for one steadying breath.

Opened them again.

Resolved.

The pilot said quietly, "First light. We hit it again at first light."

No one responded.

No one needed to.

First light wasn't when you searched for survivors.

First light was when you found what the ocean chose to give back.

Bodies, if they were lucky. Debris, if they weren't. Sometimes nothing at all.

The Dolphin banked northwest, rain streaking the windows in diagonal rivers of gray. Darkness reclaimed the inlet behind them, lightning offering one last violent glimpse of the churning mouth before swallowing it whole.

Hartley stared down through the open side window, watching the roar of black water slip beneath them. The storm had carved wild, shifting paths across the surface, and he tracked them with a grim, instinctive attention.

He'd remember this night. Whether they found anyone tomorrow or not, he'd carry it with him.

Somewhere out there, a canoe fought to survive.

And the ocean had not yet made its decision.

Chapter Sixteen

The Rescue Attempt

The storm had not merely arrived; it had descended with intent, hurling its full weight down the throat of Ocracoke Inlet as though the place had offended it. The pressure of it felt personal, vindictive, and old. Caleb felt that accusation in his bones, as if the inlet and the storm had struck some ancient bargain he was now being forced to pay for. The air around him throbbed with an old, tidal anger—one that rose from water, wind, and memory.

Sheets of rain slashed sideways across the black water, each gust breaking the surface into white shards that vanished as quickly as they formed. The wind didn't just blow—it screamed, ripping across the channel like a living thing with a personal vendetta. Each gust seemed to target the skiff in a new way, testing for the angle that would break it.

Caleb eased the skiff forward, one hand locked on the throttle, tendons drawn tight until his forearm felt carved from stone. His knuckles had blanched beneath soaked leather, stiff with cold and effort. The air tasted metallic, sharp with salt and storm electricity, and beneath the roar he sensed the low vibration of the bar—a deep, stomach-level hum like distant thunder that never quite resolved. It was a tone you didn't hear so much as absorb. A warning carved into the water itself.

He'd run this inlet a hundred times. In daylight. In calm seas. In summer squalls that only pretended to be dangerous. Even then, he held respect for the place—every local did. But tonight wasn't pretending. Tonight stripped away all familiarity, leaving something raw and unpredictable in its place.

Tonight felt different.

Older.

Meaner.

The inlet was shifting with every passing second, its sandbars seeming to appear in unseen places. The ocean rearranged itself in the dark like a creature shedding one skin for another. Channels that had existed yesterday were erased now, replaced by violent crosscurrents pulling in directions no chart could predict. What had once been a familiar route was now a battlefield, and Caleb was the trespasser.

A wave detonated against the port side, flinging icy spray across his face. The force of it made him blink hard, lashes clumping with salt. The spotlight carved a narrow pale tunnel through the dark, but beyond its reach there was nothing—no horizon, no silhouettes, only void. Even the sky felt erased, like the storm had scrubbed it clean and replaced it with a ceiling of moving black.

The engine growled beneath him, vibrating through the soles of his boots. The skiff shuddered with each gust, the hull flexing under the violence of water and wind. He nudged the throttle. Just enough. Push too hard and he'd lose control; hesitate and the next swell would shove him backward like a toy.

Caleb drew in a steady breath through his teeth, forcing his lungs open against the pressure building in his chest. The cold wet air stabbed at his throat, sharp enough to make him cough, but he swallowed it down.

For the briefest second, Jesse's face flared in his mind—then Sadie's—smiling on the ferry that morning, unaware the night would try to take her.

"Not tonight..."

The wind swallowed the words before they left him.

"I'm not losing anyone tonight."

He squared himself at the helm, feet braced, jaw set, and drove the skiff straight into the storm's open mouth.

The first true wave didn't hit so much as condemn the boat. A towering ridge of black water rose ahead without warning, a shifting wall that revealed its shape only when the spotlight caught the crest. It had shoulders—angles—height. It moved with intent. Caleb barely had time to adjust the throttle before the bow climbed steeply, his boots sliding an inch on the soaked deck. Wind shrieked over the gunnel, tearing at his drenched shirt, plastering the fabric to the lines of his back.

The skiff dropped—hammering the trough so hard his teeth snapped together. Salt flooded his tongue, adrenaline and pain mixing into a harsh metallic tang. The impact rattled up through his legs, a bone-deep shock that made his knees buckle before he locked them again.

Stay on it. Stay on it. Do not let the bow fall sideways.

He nudged the throttle forward, forcing the bow into the next swell before the current could seize the stern and twist him broadside. The inlet's cross-rip wanted exactly that—to take the boat, fold it, drag him into the bar where the storm would finish the job.

Spray knifed across the console, stinging his face. It clung to his eyelashes, blurring the world into streaks of silver and black. The spotlight jerked and trembled, fighting the storm's rage, each beam scattering into broken shards of light the moment it hit airborne spray.

The wind devoured every sound except the engine's strained growl, and even that felt muted, more vibration than noise. Caleb shifted his stance, reading the inlet by instinct alone. He felt the current thicken under the hull, sensed the subtle lift when shallow water lurked beneath, recognized the pressure of a swell rising from below rather than from the wind.

He read the water the way some men read Scripture.

Another wave slammed him broadside. The skiff lurched violently, the console striking his shoulder hard enough to make him grunt. Pain shot down his arm, but he rolled into it, muscled the wheel around, and forced the bow back before the next breaker could sweep him sideways into disaster.

Rain blurred everything.

The spotlight found only walls of foam and shadow.

His breath fogged in the cold air, each exhale snatched away by the wind before it drifted more than an inch from his lips.

And all he could think was how cold Sadie must be. How scared Jesse must be. How long the ocean had been doing this—taking what it wanted, answering to no one.

"Come on..." he muttered. "Come on, show me something... anything."

The GPS flickered again as another jolt shook the hull. Coordinates jumped, scrambled—like a heartbeat under shock. He didn't trust it now. The inlet did not want to be mapped tonight.

The current clawed at the hull—sideways, forward, sideways again—pulling him into a chaotic rhythm that felt almost intentional, like the inlet was guiding him toward a place he had no wish to go.

Through the haze—movement.

Something small, fast, and violently out of place.

A streak of neon orange.

A life jacket.

Not from his skiff.

Not meant to be here.

Not drifting idly, but tumbling in the current like it had been torn away in panic moments ago. The storm seized it, yanking it toward the open Atlantic as though claiming a prize.

Caleb's breath hitched.

For a single, crushing heartbeat he saw Sadie in that flash of orange—her hair plastered to her cheeks, her arms reaching for him, her voice lost to the wind.

He knew it wasn't her.

But the surge of terror felt real enough to cut him open.

His hands shook on the wheel. He had to force them steady.

"Hold on... just hold on..."

The inlet constricted around him like a fist. The broad throat narrowed into a violent channel where waves rose from multiple directions at once. Not clean swells—stacked angles of water colliding in the dark, jagged and unpredictable, the kind that could break a skiff in half if the timing slipped. The roar of water smashing into itself filled his ears, a chaotic percussion that drowned out even the engine.

The GPS flickered uselessly.

The spotlight trembled.

The inlet roared its warning:

You are drifting.

You are drifting.

You are drifting.

He fought back with wheel and throttle, each correction a battle against forces stronger than him. Spray blew sideways across the deck, soaking him in sheets. The stern slipped eastward—toward the bar.

He wasn't approaching it anymore.

He was on it.

A swell surged beneath the hull—huge, merciless, lifting the bow at a perilous angle. Caleb braced hard against the console as the boat climbed higher, the breaker behind him rising like a looming black wall.

"No—"

The bow crested.

Hung in a moment of terrible weightlessness. Even the wind seemed to pause, holding its breath with him.

Then the world dropped.

The wave twisted the skiff, stern sliding as the breaker collapsed sideways. Caleb threw his weight into the wheel, nudged the throttle, and forced the boat into a skidding descent down the wave's face.

For a breath, there was no water beneath him.

Only air.

Only chaos.

Then—THUD.

The hull slammed into the trough with a force that rattled bolts. Water exploded across the deck. Gear clattered. Caleb held the wheel with both hands, arms trembling with exertion, but he did not let go.

He counter-steered through the next swell, and another, dragging the skiff off the bar's death line and into deeper water. Behind him, the breaker he escaped detonated in a white explosion that blotted out the night for an instant.

Two seconds slower and the bar would have taken him. The inlet had let him go.

He didn't dare look back.

It was over. There was nothing else he could do.

It was time to go back.

The waves eased from murderous spikes into rough, punishing swells. The spotlight steadied. The storm still howled, but no longer with the intent to kill. It felt like an opponent catching its breath, reassessing.

Caleb didn't feel relief.

He felt the ache of a man who knew he hadn't reached the people he'd come for.

The harbor gathered him in slowly—rage giving way to ugly chop, to a storm-thrashed basin where masts rattled and dock lights flickered like dying candles. The water here was calmer, but full of debris—leaves, branches, foam, pieces of docks battered loose by the storm.

He tied the skiff off by muscle memory.

Turned the key.

The engine coughed, then died.

Silence fell on him like a collapse.

No voices in the dark. No one calling for help. Just the storm and his own ragged breathing.

He grabbed the radio, thumbed the switch. "Captain, this is Caleb. I'm back. Couldn't find them. Any word from the Coast Guard?"

Static. Then Riggs's voice, heavy with something worse than exhaustion.

"They called off the search, son. Ran low on fuel. They're done until first light."

Caleb's knees nearly buckled.

He sagged onto the deck, water soaking through every layer, fingers trembling from adrenaline and cold. His breath came in uneven pulls, each one tight in his chest.

Sadie's face flashed again.

Jesse's worry.

And he had not broken through.

He had not gotten to them.

Thunder rolled across the inlet, a distant echo of the violence he'd barely outrun. Caleb stared into that darkness, jaw tight, breath unsteady. The storm still raged, still ruled the night, still guarded whatever it held inside that violent throat.

"You didn't beat me," he whispered. "Not all the way."

He stood on shaking legs, stepped onto the dock, and let the rain drum down on him—cold, relentless, reminding him the night wasn't finished.

Lightning flashed beyond the harbor, revealing the inlet's silhouette like the gaping mouth of something ancient and hungry.

Hold on, he thought.

Please... just hold on a little longer.

Sadie. He'd said her name into the storm. He had to believe she'd heard him somehow.

He walked toward the ferry with no plan, no certainty—only a resolve that felt carved into his bones.

First light. That was when the Coast Guard would search again. He'd be out there with them.

He wasn't giving up on them.

His whole body ached—arms, back, ribs. The inlet had taken a lot out of him. But not everything.

Not tonight.

The storm could rage.

The inlet could judge.

The ocean could take and take and take.

But Caleb O'Neal wasn't finished.

Not until he brought them home.

Chapter Seventeen

The Confession

The ocean had erased the world.

No sky.

No horizon.

No point of reference to cling to.

Only a heaving, endless, lightless void rising and falling beneath a storm determined to swallow every remaining scrap of sound, memory, warmth, and hope.

The sea did not roar so much as it consumed. Sound flattened beneath the weight of wind and water until even the crash of waves felt distant, like a memory of noise instead of the thing itself. Somewhere far below, unseen swells heaved and twisted, reshaping the surface with every breath. The boat was nothing against that—the smallest wrong-shaped thing in a world built entirely of motion.

Far beyond the inlet—past the disappearing flicker of land lights, past the chaos Caleb was fighting, past anything resembling safety—an overturned johnboat drifted alone in the open Atlantic. It climbed and dropped with the slow, monstrous pulse of deep water, each swell lifting the little hull with a groaning effort before letting it fall in a heavy, jarring thud. The force vibrated up Boone's bones, as though the sea were knocking from below and asking how much longer he intended to hold on.

There was no sense of direction anymore. The boat had long since lost any relationship to north or south, to shore or shoal; it simply rolled wherever the long swell chose to push it. Sometimes it felt as if he was being dragged sideways down the face of some unseen ridge of water, the world tilting at a sickening angle before leveling out again. Other times the motion came from underneath, a slow lift that pretended to be gentle until it ended in a brutal drop that jarred his teeth and spine.

He didn't know anything anymore.

Time had come unhooked. Minutes, hours—those were land things, measured by clocks and sunlight and the shape of shadows. Out here there was only the stretch between breaths and the space between each new impact of wave against hull. Boone couldn't have said if he'd been clinging to the boat for ten minutes or ten years. All he knew was the ache baked into his muscles and the cold rooted into his bones.

Boone clung to the cold aluminum, arms wrapped across the slick underside. His chest was bare, skin tinted bluish from the creeping reach of hypothermia. His clothes were gone—ripped away by waves or peeled off in blind panic when they dragged him under. The water had taken everything from him except the thin, unraveling thread of his will to live.

The aluminum leeched heat from him with a relentless hunger. Every place his skin touched metal felt carved out, hollowed by contact. His forearms burned where the jagged edge of a rivet had already chewed the skin raw, but even that pain was dimming, slipping further from sharp awareness into something distant and muffled.

His teeth chattered in a rhythm sharp enough to crack enamel. His fingers curled awkwardly around the metal, stiffening in place, refusing every command he sent down his arms. His breath fogged weakly in the cold wind, each fragile puff torn away instantly.

Air scraped in and out of him in short, uneven pulls. He could hear the hollow rattle in his chest, a wet hitch at the end of each inhale where cold and panic had worn his lungs thin. Somewhere in the back of his mind, the rational part that still tried to name things, he recognized what was happening—body temperature dropping, muscles failing, thoughts coming slower, like they had to fight through thick syrup to reach the front of his mind. But the naming didn't help. Knowing the word hypothermia did nothing to stop it.

Darkness pressed in from all directions.

An absolute blackness.

It was not the soft dark of a mountain night, with its distant porch lights and stars shining through gaps in the trees. This was a heavier thing, an old, sea-deep black that felt layered and alive. Every shift of cloud swallowed what little reflection there was on the water, turning the surface from charcoal to ink to the color of nothing at all. Boone's eyes strained against it, searching for any hint of shape or distance, but the world kept arriving as the same blank, unbroken void.

Out here, there was no difference between ocean and sky—only shifting shadow, moving cold, and the endless slap of water against the overturned hull.

Sometimes, when lightning flickered far inside the clouds, he thought he could almost see the edge of a wave or the ghost of a horizon. By the time his brain tried to fix the image in place, it was gone again, leaving him with only the memory of shape and the churn of his own disorientation. Up and down traded places so often his stomach could no longer tell which direction falling was.

A wave smacked across the boat and slammed into Boone's face with brutal force. Saltwater flooded his nose and mouth. He gagged, coughed, nearly lost his grip. His hands found the metal again at the last second—numb fingers sliding across wet aluminum, almost giving way.

His sinuses burned. Every breath came with the taste of the ocean ground into it, a harsh, mineral scrape that made him feel as if he'd swallowed the whole inlet. Water ran from his nose into his mouth, and for a terrifying instant he didn't know which way to force it—whether to spit or swallow or just let it go. His body decided for him in a spasmodic cough that left him dizzy and weaker than before.

"Oh God... oh God..."

The whisper escaped him, thin and wavering, ripped away by wind before it even reached his own ears.

His voice sounded wrong in his own head, soft and childlike, as if it belonged to someone much younger calling from somewhere far away. There was no echo, no reassuring bounce of sound off trees or buildings. The words simply vanished into the gale, erased as cleanly as footprints at the tide line.

No strength left to shout.

No bravado to mask fear.

No jokes to ease the truth.

Only the raw, unfiltered terror of a man alone in the open sea.

He had always been loud when it came to fear, quick with a laugh or a shove or a wisecrack to bend the moment away from whatever frightened him. On the water back home, he could fill an entire day with noise—stories, curses, trash talk—anything to keep silence from settling too heavily. Now there was nothing left to throw at it. The storm was louder, and the sea was older, and both of them had more to say than he ever would.

"I'm sorry... I'm sorry for everything..."

The words spilled out before he could stop them, coming not from courage but from the deep vulnerability hypothermia carved into every part of him.

They didn't feel rehearsed. There was no speech in his head, no carefully stacked list of things he'd meant to say someday. The sentences came jagged and unfinished, fragments of remorse bumping into each other on the way out. Each syllable rasped over his tongue like something that had been waiting there a long time, heavy and sour, finally given permission to move.

Lightning ripped the sky open. For one suspended moment, the world froze in cold white light—Boone's trembling lips, glassy eyes, and the swollen darkness surrounding him. A snapshot of a man out of excuses.

The light etched everything in sharp, merciless detail. He saw the muscles in his forearms standing out like ropes, the blue tinge along his knuckles, the raw places where skin had been scrubbed away by the constant friction of metal and salt. The wave tops around him glowed ghost-pale, their edges lit in a serrated halo before the dark slammed back in with a concussive crack of thunder that seemed to arrive inside his skull.

"I shouldn't've taken that money from the church... God, I stole from a church... I shouldn't've lied to Jesse... And Sadie... God... I treated her like she didn't matter..."

The storm didn't pause to listen.

It had no interest in mercy.

The words were snatched from his mouth and shredded, the wind cutting across them at an angle that made the sound break apart even as he spoke. It struck him as almost right that it happened that way. Lies had once come easy to him, neat and smooth and well-aimed. The truth, when he finally tried to speak it, didn't hold together at all.

A sideways wave punched into the hull, knocking Boone clean underwater. Salt burned his throat. He kicked weakly, broke the surface with a gasp that sounded like drowning already in progress.

For a heartbeat beneath the surface, there was a different kind of silence—pressure-thick, heavy, a muffled roar that made the storm above feel strangely distant. The cold there was more complete, a full-body grip that squeezed his ribs and clawed up the back of his neck. When his head broke free again, the night came rushing back all at once—wind, rain, and the grinding slap of water on aluminum colliding with the burning in his lungs.

He clawed for the boat.

Once.

Twice.

Caught it on the third try.

His hands felt clumsy, as if someone had wrapped them in thick gloves he couldn't remember putting on. The distance between his fingertips and the hull seemed to stretch and shrink without warning, the boat jerking away and then lurching closer again with every rise and fall of the swell. When his fingers finally hooked the edge, relief came not as a burst of triumph but as a dull, stunned disbelief that he had managed it again.

His arms felt distant, detached—like they belonged to someone else.

"I was jealous... I was so jealous..."

The confession ripped out of him, the storm peeling away every lie he'd wrapped around himself.

The word jealous tasted more bitter than the seawater. It scraped up memories he'd tried hard not to look at—nights watching Jesse say the right thing without seeming to try, watching Sadie see past her own hurt to someone else's, watching the two of them make choices he told himself he'd make too, if life ever gave him the same chances. Only life had given him chances. He'd just diverted them, spent them on shortcuts and half-truths and easy exits.

"They're better than me... always have been... better hearts... better people..."

His muscles seized, then sagged into a shaking rhythm that felt more mechanical than conscious. His voice slurred, thick as though speaking through cloth.

The words blurred together at the edges, syllables sticking to each other, but he kept forcing them out anyway. Maybe no one would ever hear them. Maybe the storm would carry them no farther than his own ears. But the saying of them mattered in some small, strange way—as if admitting the truth aloud might leave a mark somewhere that outlived him, even if it was only on the inside of his own fading mind.

"I should've... listened—Jesse told me... Sadie told me... but I thought I knew better..."

Truth didn't arrive as some grand revelation. It came quietly, in the spaces between waves, as he replayed conversations he had brushed off, warnings he'd laughed at, the look Sadie had given him that time she'd gone quiet instead of arguing back. He could see Jesse's jaw tightening when Boone pushed too far, the patience there stretched thin but still holding. They had tried to give him something steadier than impulse to stand on. He had kicked it out from under himself every time.

"I ain't the man I thought I was..."

His head sagged toward his chest as another tremor overtook him. The shaking wasn't frantic anymore—it was slowing, the body's last desperate attempt to create heat. His hearing dulled, muffled by the creeping numbness closing in around his skull. The world sounded underwater even when he was above it.

The edges of sound grew fuzzy. Thunder became a low, rolling hum; even the slap of water against the hull lost its sharpness, turning into a steady, distant thud. Boone's own heartbeat, once a frantic drum in his ears, now felt far away, as if it belonged to someone floating near him instead of inside his own chest.

A memory flickered—warm, impossible.

Jesse laughing on the riverbank back home.

Sadie chasing fireflies, calling his name.

A younger Boone—strong, fearless, stupid—believing storms only happened to other people.

The scenes came not as full recollections, but as piercing fragments—Jesse's wet hair plastered to his forehead after they'd flipped a raft on the river, Sadie's bare feet kicking up sparks of light as she tore across a summer yard with a mason jar in her hand, the three of them collapsed on a patch of cool grass after, talking about where they'd go and what they'd do once the world got big enough to hold them. They had said things like always and no matter what and all the way to the ocean, their voices full of a certainty that now felt almost cruel.

"And God... I didn't protect 'em... I should've... I should've taken care of my friends..."

He didn't even know if they were still alive. The canoe had vanished in the dark hours ago. They could be gone already. Because of him.

His chest locked up in a sudden freeze from the inside out. He gasped when it released, dragging in a ragged breath.

The guilt cut sharper than the cold ever had. It threaded back through recent choices and old patterns alike, stitching them together into something he could finally see clearly. He had been so busy guarding his pride, his image, his shortcuts, that he hadn't guarded the people who had trusted him. That knowledge sat heavier than the weight of the ocean on his shoulders, heavier than the sky.

"Tell Jesse... tell Sadie... I want them to know... I love 'em... I really do... I just never knew how to tell them..."

Another swell rose beneath the overturned boat. The hull lurched, flinging Boone sideways. His grip slipped—fingers skidding across the metal. For one moment, he hung suspended between the boat and the black void beneath him.

The world narrowed to that sliver of distance—the measure of his life boiled down to the space between his fingers and the aluminum. He could feel gravity tugging at him, feel the cold sucking at his legs, promising a different kind of quiet if he would just let go. His shoulders screamed as his body stretched, every joint protesting the strain.

He lunged.

Caught the edge again—barely.

His knuckles whitened.

His arms screamed.

His strength evaporated.

He couldn't feel his legs.

Could barely feel his arms.

The lower half of his body might as well have belonged to the sea now. He knew his legs were there because the water still moved against them, but there was no clear line where his body ended and the ocean began. He was more aware of the weight of his own torso dragging at his shoulders than of anything below his waist. His hands had become the only points that seemed to exist, two small, desperate anchors keeping him from slipping fully into the dark.

"God... I want to be a better man... If You let me live... I'll be a better man... I swear... I promise... I— I promise..."

His voice wavered between sob and whisper, swallowed instantly by the wind.

Then, from somewhere deep—a place he'd buried so long ago he'd forgotten it existed—his grandmother's voice rose up. Sunday mornings on her porch. Her hand on his head. Teaching him words he hadn't understood.

"Create in me a clean heart, O God..." The words came out broken, barely a whisper. "...and renew a right spirit within me."

He said it again. And again. Each time weaker. Each time more true.

The vow came out broken, part request, part promise, riddled with all the times he had promised change before and failed to follow through. But this was different. This wasn't his promise. This was hers—passed down, planted, waiting for the night he'd finally need it.

The tremors came slower.

Duller.

Colder.

Each breath drifted out in smaller clouds—each one fainter than the last, each one a step closer to slipping beneath.

Somewhere in the numb distance of his limbs, he understood that this was the part where most people stopped fighting. The body, worn past sense, began to confuse cold with warmth, heaviness with rest. Thoughts untied from each other and floated loose. Boone sensed the edge of that surrender like the lip of a cliff beneath his heels. Part of him wanted to step off, to let the ache in his muscles and the burn in his lungs fall away into nothing. Another part clung stubbornly, the same hardheaded streak that had driven him into bad decisions now refusing to let go when it finally mattered most.

"Please... please don't let this be the end... let me fix what I messed up... let me make things right..."

He thought of Jesse pulling him from fights.

Of Sadie patching cuts on his hands even after he'd made her cry.

Of the three of them as kids—barefoot, dreaming big, believing they were invincible.

Jesse's hand on his shoulder, firm enough to hold him back without making a show of it. Sadie's brow furrowed as she dabbed antiseptic onto split knuckles, her voice soft but edged with frustration and care. The way they had all walked side by side down rutted roads that felt like runways leading toward something brighter. Those memories were the only warm things left to him, tiny coals banked deep in the cold.

He thought of forgiveness.

Of second chances.

Of becoming someone worth saving.

The ideas felt too big to hold in his mind, but they hovered there anyway, fragile as the pale breath drifting from his lips. He didn't know what a better man looked like, not really—not beyond the vague outline of someone who told the truth, who didn't run, who showed up when it counted. But he knew Jesse and Sadie deserved that man, whether or not he ever finished becoming him.

The ocean lifted him again.

Dropped him again.

The rhythm slowed—like the heartbeat of something ancient growing tired.

Edges softened.

The cold no longer stung—it soothed, inviting him to let go.

His eyelids barely lifted.

"And God... please... don't leave me alone... don't leave me here to die..."

The storm weakened—not from mercy, but exhaustion. Wind softened to a low moan. The ocean's fury ebbed into a massive, weary roll.

Without the constant assault of wind and spray, there was more room for the quiet to creep in, for the awareness of how far he was from anyone who knew his name. The boat rose and fell in long, rolling arcs, as if the sea itself were breathing slower now, content to hold him rather than shake him loose.

The overturned johnboat drifted on that deep, endless blackness.

Up.

Down.

Up.

Down.

Just Boone.

The dark.

And the cold.

His final whispered prayer carried across the sea until even the night swallowed it whole.

Chapter Eighteen

The Long Night

The storm had passed, but the ocean had not forgiven them.

Its anger had only changed shape.

A fragile quiet settled over the water—the kind that comes after something violent exhausts itself. The surface rolled in heavy, muscular swells, each rise and fall echoing the storm's memory. Even without thunder, Jesse felt an invisible weight on his chest, as though the world hadn't fully healed.

What had been a white-fanged chaos was now a slow, tidal resentment moving beneath them. The air still carried the metallic sting of lightning, a ghost of what had shredded the sky.

Jesse felt a faint vibration through his forearms pressed to the cold fiberglass—not rage anymore, but something older and quieter. A presence the sea kept only after the darkness settled. Sadie felt it too; her breathing turned shallow, as if the night became deeper with every hour that passed.

A long, unbroken wind swept across the Atlantic. Waves slapped the overturned canoe—hollow, rhythmic impacts echoing like a merciless countdown. Each thud vibrated through the hull and into their bones: not yet, not yet, not yet.

Time warped with the sound. Warmth, land, Boone's voice—everything before the storm drifted into distant memory. Jesse watched his breath vanish the instant it left his mouth, torn away by the wind.

The canoe rose and fell in long, shuddering lifts. No horizon. No lights. Only the slick curve of the overturned hull and the endless dark.

Without a horizon or anchor point, the swells felt alive, tugging at them as if deciding whether to take them now or later. Sadie's movements slowed, reduced to faint, conserving shifts. Scout's trembling was the only sign they weren't completely alone.

Jesse and Sadie clung to the canoe, bodies shaking so violently their teeth clattered like stones. Their fingers burned, numbed, then drifted into something beyond sensation. Between them, Scout scraped weakly along the slick aluminum.

All light had vanished without ceremony.

The deepness of night was upon them—starless and absolute.

Sadie curled her fingers around Scout's wet fur.

"Scout... oh God... Scout..."

"You're doing good, Sadie," Jesse whispered, though his own voice shook. "Just hold on."

A crooked swell lifted them sharply. Jesse braced, but the wave struck before he was ready, breaking over them and flipping his grip. Salt rushed into his lungs as the world inverted in cold, roaring static. Instinct dragged him back to the surface. He clawed for the canoe and found it.

"It's so dark, Jesse... we're not gonna make it..." Sadie whispered. "Boone...?"

"Boone!!" he shouted.

Sadie's voice trailed after his—thin, desperate.

"Boone!!"

Their cries vanished into the dark.

"We have to hold on till morning," Jesse said.

"What if there's no morning?"

"There will be," he whispered. "I swear."

Time dissolved. The night thickened, sinking deeper into itself. Jesse's eyelids sagged again and again; each time he jolted awake, terrified sleep meant death. Sadie's breaths came in shallow, uneven bursts.

Then—a slip, a scrape.

Scout's paws faltered.

"Scout... Scout, stay with me..." Sadie begged.

"She's slipping, Sadie."

A tilt—barely anything—and Scout slid off the canoe.

Moments ago he'd been pressed against them, alive, shivering. Jesse struggled to reach her.

"NO! SCOUT!!"

Sadie's scream tore through the night—raw, jagged.

Jesse lunged, arms sweeping blindly through the dark. Scout wasn't just a dog. She was woven into their lives, their childhood, their years on the water. Losing her felt impossible, a violation of something pure.

Sadie clawed through the waves, sobbing in broken gasps.

"Scout!! Scout!!"

A swell shoved Jesse sideways, but he fought through it, searching for any sign of white fur.

Then—a flicker.

Scout paddled weakly, strokes slowing, her pale body rising and disappearing in the dark. She slipped out of sight entirely.

For one heartbeat, Scout's eyes found Sadie's—calm, trusting, as if to say it was okay. Then the swell took him.

She was gone.

Sadie reached out with trembling hands.

"Scout... baby... please..."

Her voice shattered.

Tears stung Jesse's eyes, hot against the cold. He could see Scout's tired, trusting gaze in his mind.

He tried to speak, but nothing left his throat.

Sadie made a sound Jesse had never heard from her before—a raw, broken note from somewhere ancient and wounded.

Sadie collapsed against the canoe, sobbing so violently Jesse feared she might slip under with the next wave.

He pressed his forehead to the hull.

I should've saved her. I should've held her tighter.

When he looked up, Sadie was staring into the water.

"Jesse... there's something under us..."

Her voice carried no fear—only conviction.

The darkness below shifted—not like water, but like a curtain parting. A faint, impossible glow emerged, revealing a shape beneath the surface.

A woman's face drifted upward, hair spreading like pale kelp. Softened features. The familiar downturn of the mouth.

"Mom...?" Sadie whispered.

Her mother's eyes opened—not filled with sorrow, but with warmth. A smile Sadie hadn't seen since she was fifteen. A hand lifted toward her, not reaching, not pulling. Just offering.

You're okay, baby. You're going to be okay.

Sadie's breath caught.

Then the image dissolved—replaced by another figure rising from the dark.

Jesse.

But older.

Hair streaked with silver. Lines carved into his face. Eyes heavy with years Sadie hadn't lived to see. His mouth moved beneath the water, shaping soundless words:

Swim to shore... swim to shore...

Sadie's breath hitched.

But this wasn't just Jesse grown old. The jaw. The eyes. The way he held himself even in stillness.

The man from the photograph. The name on the gravestone she'd seen on Howard Street, glowing in the lantern light: Jesse Dixon. 1872–1899. Died in the line of duty. U.S. Life-Saving Service.

He'd died here. In these waters. A storm in 1899, saving strangers who never knew his name.

And now he was telling her how to save his blood.

Swim to shore.

"Jesse—" she gasped, gripping his arm. "We have to swim to shore."

Jesse's blood went cold. Her eyes weren't tracking right. She was staring past him, through him, at something in the water that wasn't there. He'd heard about hypothermia doing this—the confusion, the visions, the quiet slide toward death.

This was it. He was losing her.

"We can't, Sadie." He fought to keep his voice steady. "There is no shore."

"There is," she whispered, her gaze still fixed on something beneath the surface. "He's telling me. Swim to shore."

"Who's telling you? Sadie—" His voice cracked. He grabbed her face with numb hands, forced her to look at him. "Stay with me. There's no one there. It's just the cold. You have to stay with me."

But her eyes drifted back to the water.

"He's here, Jesse. He's been with us the whole time."

"Who?"

She didn't answer. The vision extended a trembling hand. Sadie felt a swell of grief—for a future lost, for a man who drowned saving others over a century ago, for a bloodline that had carried his courage all the way to this moment.

The face beneath the water held her gaze one moment longer.

Then it dissolved.

Sadie swayed, grip weakening.

Jesse cupped her face in his freezing hands.

"There's nothing there. Look at me. Look right at me."

Her gaze lifted, the visions fading like mist.

She rested her cheek against the canoe.

"I got her for my eighth birthday...now Scout's gone!"

Her voice thinned to a whisper.

"I'm tired... Jesse... I can't..."

Something inside him broke.

He pressed his forehead to hers.

"Sadie. Look at me. Please."

Her eyelids fluttered.

"I can't lose you," he whispered. "Not you. Not ever."

"I should've told you this a long time ago... I love you."

Twelve years of silence. Twelve years of watching her and saying nothing. If this was the end, she deserved to know.

"I've loved you since we were twelve years old..."

Her breath caught.

"You have to stay with me. Because I love you. I've loved you my whole life."

"...Jesse..."

All those years. All those moments she'd wondered. He'd been carrying this the whole time, just like her.

She found his eyes in the dark.

"I love you too. I always have."

The words hung between them—fragile and true.

A deeper breath moved through her.

"Sadie. Remember the French Broad? That day we flipped the canoe?"

"What did you say?"

A pause.

A flicker.

"Nothing can stop us..."

"Say it again."

"I can't..."

"Yes you can. Nothing... can stop us..."

"Nothing can stop us..."

Her grip strengthened.

Something flickered back into her eyes. Fight.

Jesse couldn't feel his hands anymore. Couldn't feel much of anything except Sadie beside him.

"That's the Sadie Lynn Whittaker I know."

"For Scout," he whispered. "And for me."

"Okay... for you... and for Scout..."

***

The night seemed endless, but Sadie thought she saw a pale glimmer of light appeared on the horizon.

"That's land..." she murmured.

Sadie's breath caught. The shore. It had been there all along.

"Jesse." Her voice cracked. "He was right."

"What?"

"The ghost... he told me. Swim to shore." She turned to him. "You said there was no shore. But I believe there is. He knew. He told me"

Jesse stared at what appeared to be a pale hint of a light. She'd seen it before he had.

"Sadie... what are you saying?"

"Later," she whispered. "I'll tell you everything. Later. When we get to land."

They didn't know if it was the island. The currents could have pulled them parallel to the beach all night, miles down the coast. But it looked like a light. It was enough.

"We have to swim," she said.

Their eyes met. No words needed. They both knew what had to happen next.

They released the canoe and slipped into the water.

The hull drifted away behind them—their only shelter all night, gone in seconds.

The cold struck like knives.

Each stroke a battle.

Side by side, they swam toward hope.

Jesse's limbs locked with every movement. Sadie drifted in and out of rhythm, her legs trailing until she willed them into motion again.

"Sadie... stay with me..." he rasped.

The faint glow ahead was barely more than suggestion, but it tethered them—something real to swim toward.

The water grew heavier the farther they went. Swells lifted and dropped them in slow, indifferent rhythms. A wave slapped Sadie across the mouth; she coughed, breath thin and shaky.

"Jesse... I don't... I don't know if I can..."

"You can," he said, kicking harder despite the fire burning through him. "I'm right here."

He brushed her arm with his fingertips—just enough to steady her stroke. She lifted her head and took a fuller breath.

The faint glimmer of light brightened by a fraction.

"It's land" Sadie whispered.

"It is," Jesse said. "I believe you."

Time blurred—only the rhythm of limbs fighting water, the ache in their bones, the cold chewing toward their cores. Jesse's thoughts fractured—Boone laughing in the canoe, Scout chasing foam, Sadie on the ferry deck—

—her face in the cupola, leaning toward him, the kiss that almost happened—

flashes of memory he couldn't stop.

She dipped too low; seawater filled her mouth. She coughed violently.

"Stay up," he growled. "Stay up."

Sadie rolled sideways, stroke faltering. Jesse forced himself toward her and braced her back until she straightened again.

"I'm here," he whispered. "Sadie, I'm right here."

He found her hand beneath the water and held it. Cold fingers locking together.

She made a small sound—half sob, half breath—but she kept swimming.

The sky had lightened—slow, but real.

A faint smear of light sharpened in the distance.

Maybe a mile. Maybe less.

It didn't matter.

They were alive.

"Sadie," Jesse said, voice hoarse, "Don't give up."

Her lips parted in exhausted hope.

"For Scout," she whispered.

Sixteen years. She wasn't going to let Scout down now.

"For Scout," Jesse echoed.

Somewhere behind them, the sea held their friend.

Their bodies had stopped making sense hours ago. This was something else—something that refused to quit.

Together—barely holding above the water—they swam toward the faint light... and what they hoped was shore.

The ocean had not forgiven them. But it was letting them go.

Chapter Nineteen

The Covenant

Morning crept over the Atlantic, a pale, washed-out light bleeding across an endless stretch of uneasy water. After the storm's fury, the world looked fragile — the sky thin, tentative, the sea rolling in long, tired swells like a massive creature trying to settle after a night of rage. The faint glow didn't warm so much as reveal, pulling soft outlines from the gloom: ridges of waves rising and falling like labored breathing.

The ocean heaved beneath the dim sky, restless but no longer murderous. The wind still carried the storm's dying scream — stretched thin across the horizon — but weary now. It moved with a kind of reluctant persistence.

Boone floated at the center of it all, a small, shivering shape clinging to the overturned johnboat. Hours had stripped him down to something elemental: a body and a will. The night had scrubbed away everything else. Even the memory of warmth felt distant—firelight and voices and solid ground from some other life.

His bare chest was mottled blue and purple, skin marbled by cold. His lips were cracked, his fingertips waxy and white where they hooked around the hull. His hands barely felt attached — stiff claws at the ends of his arms. Occasionally a tremor ran through him, a sharp, involuntary jerk from somewhere deep inside.

Time had slipped away. There were no minutes or hours anymore, just dark water, shock, and the quiet terror of believing he might be the only living thing left on the ocean. The sky offered no comfort; it had watched him all night with a blank expression.

Jesse.

Sadie.

Scout.

Where was Scout? The dog had been on the canoe with them.

Their names drifted through him. He saw them in lightning flashes — Jesse's face contorted with fear, Sadie's hair plastered to her cheeks, the canoe disappearing into white water. He'd shouted until his voice tore, and then there had been only wind. In the gray light, their faces slipped in and out of focus each time he blinked.

If they're gone... that's on me.

The thought no longer came with anger, only weight—a sinking heaviness that pressed deeper than cold or exhaustion, settling into a place he couldn't numb.

His head sagged. Every breath rattled, thin and ghostlike. The world blurred around the edges, softening into indistinct shapes that rocked with the motion of the waves.

It would be so easy to let go.

His fingers twitched, loosening for a heartbeat. The hull shifted beneath him, the ocean whispering sleep in its slow, hypnotic rise and fall. Boone's eyelids drifted halfway shut.

One more wave. That's all it would take. He could stop fighting and let the cold finish what it started.

Then, a new vibration threaded through the air — mechanical, rhythmic.

Rotor blades.

At first, Boone thought it was another hallucination. There had been plenty during the night — voices from long-dead memory, his father calling from a riverbank, Jesse laughing somewhere just out of reach. But this sound grew clearer, steadier. It vibrated across the surface of the water.

Wup-wup-wup-wup.

He forced his eyes open.

A Coast Guard helicopter swept low over the ocean, its shadow skimming across the swells. Rotor wash churned spirals of spray as the aircraft banked into position, slicing a clean path through the morning haze. The motion of it — deliberate, controlled — pierced through the fog in his mind like a flare.

Inside the cockpit, a pilot's voice crackled over comms — clipped, focused, urgent.

"We've got a visual. One survivor — clinging to an overturned vessel."

Boone didn't hear the words, only the vibration of a human presence carried across the water. He squinted up into the brightness and motion, mind struggling to accept the reality of shape and color. The bright orange hue of the aircraft seemed impossibly vivid.

Below the helicopter, the johnboat lay belly-up — a small scar of white in an infinite gray.

Clinging to its slick underside was Boone.

He looked barely human — skin drawn tight over sharp angles, arms shivering in violent spasms, head lolling with exhaustion. Hypothermia pulled him in and out of consciousness like a tide. Each breath was work he no longer had the strength for. The cold had hollowed him, carved him out until only a thin thread of life remained.

For a moment, the helicopter hovered above him like a second sun — warm, bright, impossible.

"Dropping swimmer."

The rescue swimmer descended in a controlled rappel, a dark silhouette against the pale sky. Booted feet hit open air, then spray and plunged smoothly into the rolling waves with practiced purpose. The contrast between his strength and Boone's limp endurance felt almost surreal.

Rotor wash hammered the water, blasting chaotic rings outward as the swimmer fought through the chop toward Boone's drifting refuge. Every stroke deliberate, efficient.

Boone lifted his head a fraction, muscles screaming. The world swung and blurred — hull, sky, orange-and-black figure. For one fleeting moment, he thought it might be Jesse coming out of the storm for him.

His lips parted, but only broken fragments escaped.

"J—... Sadie..."

The swimmer reached the johnboat, bracing himself against a swell. One look at Boone's color and unfocused eyes told him everything.

A human face, after all those hours of darkness and water.

"Hey!" he shouted over the roar. "I've got you. Stay with me!"

Boone heard only parts — got you — but something inside him softened. The stubborn refusal to die that had carried him through the night loosened its grip, replaced by a fragile sense of relief.

He sagged forward as the swimmer's arm slid around him, pulling him against a steady, anchored form that would not be swallowed by the sea.

The harness came next — straps under Boone's arms, across his chest, cinched tight. His vision wavered, narrowing into a tunnel of gray and movement.

Above them, the winch cable hummed.

"Ready for pickup!" the swimmer signaled.

The line tightened.

Boone lifted from the water — slowly, weightlessly — spinning in small circles as the helicopter reeled him upward. Spray trailed from his limbs.

His body broke the surface for the last time.

Then he rose higher.

Away from the ocean.

Away from the night.

The johnboat shrank beneath him, a white smear on an infinite gray canvas. No sign of a canoe. No familiar faces.

Please... let them be out there. Please...

The thought flickered as his head rolled back and his eyes slipped shut.

Warmth hit him like a shock.

He'd begged for this. Begged God not to leave him alone in the cold. And here it was.

Red instrument lights. Metallic walls. The hum of machinery. The sudden, almost painful heat of blankets and warming packs pressed to his chest and under his arms. The contrast made his skin sting as sensation returned.

Boone lay on the deck, wrapped in foil and wool, breath rattling in uneven bursts. Steam rose faintly from his skin as his body struggled to understand warmth again. The air inside the cabin tasted like metal and adrenaline.

A crewman knelt beside him, bracing against the helicopter's sway. His gloved hands moved with practiced urgency — checking Boone's airway, feeling for a pulse, adjusting the oxygen mask hovering near Boone's chapped lips. His voice carried calm authority.

"Core temp's low," the crewman called. "Packs tight. Keep him talking."

Another crew member tucked blankets tight around Boone's shoulders, trying to trap the fragile heat blooming beneath the layers. Boone flinched at the touch.

Boone's eyelids fluttered. The world blurred and swam — red light, silver foil, the dark outline of uniforms. The rotor noise vibrated through the metal floor, a constant mechanical heartbeat.

"You're lucky to be alive," the crewman said, steady but warm.

Alive.

The word drifted through Boone. It felt foreign, as if it belonged to someone else.

His lips cracked as he tried to form sound.

"...thank you..."

It came out as a rasp, barely audible.

"What's that?" the crewman leaned closer.

Boone swallowed, throat raw.

"...thank you..."

A single tear slid from the corner of his eye, leaving a cold track down his cheek. Pain or relief—he couldn't tell.

He said it again, breath trembling.

"...thank you... thank you..."

The crewman rested a gloved hand on his shoulder, grounding him.

"Hey — we've got you. You're safe now."

Safe.

His body didn't believe it yet. Muscles were still braced for the next wave, the next pull downward. Inside, he was still on the hull calling Jesse's name into nothing.

He'd made promises in the dark. To God. To himself.

His grandmother's words had come to him out there—he couldn't remember when. Create in me a clean heart, O God, and renew a right spirit within me. He'd said it over and over until the words became a pulse, a rhythm to hold onto when everything else let go.

Now he was alive to keep that promise—or break it.

He forced his eyes to focus.

"J—" His voice cracked. "My... friends..."

"Easy," the crewman soothed. "We'll get the whole story when we land. Right now you just breathe."

Boone tried to nod. The motion cost him everything.

Jesse.

Sadie.

Scout.

Their faces flickered behind his eyes, overlapping. His chest tightened again, the fear returning sharper now that he had space to feel it.

They have to be alive. They have to.

Outside, the helicopter banked toward the coastline. Through the open door, land was still distant — a pale, uneven smudge — but closer with every pass of the rotors. The world below sharpened: the white crease of breakers, the thin line of dunes, the muted greens of wind-flattened brush.

Another crewman leaned out the door, scanning the water.

"Sea state's rough. A lot of debris. We'll log position and relay — check for missing vessels."

Boone heard only fragments — debris... missing — but they lodged deep.

Missing meant they hadn't found them yet. Missing meant they might never find them at all.

He tried to lift his head, but the medic pressed him back.

"Lie still."

Boone closed his eyes. Behind them, he saw not the johnboat but a canoe drifting in darkness—Jesse and Sadie clinging to it.

"...thank you..." he whispered again.

The crewman squeezed his shoulder.

"You're gonna be all right. Seen colder guys than you make it. You're tough."

Boone didn.t feel tough.

The night had scraped him down to bone and confession. Whatever was left, he'd have to rebuild.

But maybe surviving meant he had one more chance to set things right.

The coastline sharpened into dunes and brush as the helicopter flew over the banks. Waves crashed in long white rows.

He didn't recognize the shoreline. The currents had carried him somewhere he'd never been before.

From up here, the inlet looked calm... almost harmless. Boone's breath hitched.

That inlet had nearly killed all three of them. It didn't get to look peaceful now.

Boone's breath shuddered out as he stared toward shore.

You made it. Find out if they did.

The helicopter angled toward its landing zone, engines humming like something steady and alive.

Wrapped in foil and wool, Boone lay between the world that nearly claimed him and the one waiting for him.

"...thank you..." he murmured one final time, to the crew, to the morning, to whatever thread had held when everything else broke.

If they were alive, he'd spend the rest of his life earning it. If they weren't—he didn't know how he'd survive that.

The helicopter carried him toward land — and toward everything that would come next.

Chapter Twenty

Together at Dawn

Dawn eased over Portsmouth Island, as though wary of waking what the night had nearly claimed. It began as a faint line of washed-out color along the horizon — a pale bruise stretching across the rim of the world. Light seeped rather than rose, pressing gently into the dark. Pink, gray, the first suggestion of gold.

The air held a tremor of memory. Even the faintest breeze carried a kind of hesitation, gliding low over the sand as if mindful of disturbing whatever the storm hadn't claimed.

The storm had passed, but the world it left behind was hollow.

Pale light spread across a long stretch of beach—remote, windswept, untouched except by tide. The sand was dark with moisture, its ripples sharply etched where the night wind had combed it clean. Seaweed lay in tangled ropes along the high-water line. Shells glinted like fragments of bone in the shallow tide.

A faint mist skimmed the surface of the beach, lifting and falling with the breath of the morning. The ocean's long, tired pulse smoothed the shoreline in soft strokes.

The air felt thin, depleted.

Far from the old village, this beach felt forgotten — a place where time hesitated, waiting for the tide to decide who lived and who didn't.

An old RV perched near the dunes, its paint sun-faded to the color of worn bone, its seams streaked with rust. A canvas tent sagged beside it, bowed under gear and weather.

Wind whispered around the RV's corners. The campsite felt lived-in, sturdy—a pocket of human persistence.

Fishing rods leaned against the bumper. A cooler sat half-sunk in the sand beside a tackle box whose hinges had long given up.

A small fire crackled inside a ring of driftwood, flickering softly in the pale air.

The old fisherman — early seventies, lined and weathered by decades of tide — poured coffee from a tin pot into a dented metal cup. His movements carried the unthinking rhythm of an ancient routine.

He lifted the cup, breathed in the steam, and turned toward the horizon. The ocean murmured in strange, unsettled cadences. He listened without effort.

He sipped.

The morning quiet wrapped around him like a familiar coat. The fire's warmth on his shins, the cool air on his cheeks, the steady beat of waves — all of it formed the same pattern he'd known since boyhood. And yet today something felt different.

Then —

Movement in the surf.

Not the rhythm of waves. Not the skitter of birds.

Something else.

He lowered his cup, eyes narrowing.

Two figures staggered out of the water.

They'd made it. Somehow, they'd made it.

Jesse and Sadie.

At first, they were only silhouettes in the soft haze. As dawn strengthened, their outlines sharpened: soaked, trembling, barely upright. Their legs collapsed beneath them every few steps.

A cold prickle ran across the fisherman's skin. He had seen shipwreck survivors before — had pulled men from storms and found others too late — and there was a certain look the sea left on the living. These two wore it plainly.

The inlet. It had to be.

"My gracious..." the fisherman breathed.

His cup fell into the sand unnoticed.

He broke into a hurried stride, boots sinking deep.

"Lord above... you two look like you walked out of a grave."

Behind him, the RV door creaked open.

His wife appeared — gray hair tousled, sweater sleeves pulled low over her hands. She took one look and disappeared back inside. Seconds later she reemerged with two thick wool blankets pressed to her chest.

She hurried after her husband.

"Are you hurt? Can you walk?" the fisherman asked, voice firm but gentle.

Jesse didn't answer. His knees buckled, dropping him into the sand.

He'd held on for hours. Now his body finally had permission to stop.

Sadie fell beside him, breath shallow, face pale, her body shuddering.

Their cheeks were the color of old marble, drained of warmth.

Their skin carried an eerie bluish tint. Salt clung to their lashes. Their hair hung in stiff, tangled ropes.

The fisherman wrapped Sadie with steady hands. His wife draped the second blanket around Jesse, guiding his trembling fingers to pull it close.

"You're safe now, honey," she said softly. "Whatever happened out there, it's over."

"You two came outta nowhere... what in the world happened?" the fisherman said softly. The couple helped them rise — slow, careful — and guided them toward the warmth of the fire.

Heat washed over them in sharp waves, almost hostile after so many hours of cold. Jesse hissed as sensation surged through his limbs — sharp, needling pain as circulation returned.

His arms twitched involuntarily.

Sadie trembled so violently she could barely grip the blanket. Steam lifted from her clothes in thin wisps.

No one spoke for a long moment.

The fire crackled.

The waves hissed.

Wind combed gently through the dunes.

Jesse and Sadie breathed in shallow, uneven gulps.

The fire warmed her skin, but her mind was still in the water. Still searching.

"Jesse..." she whispered, voice fracturing. "You think Boone's out there somewhere? You think he's alive?"

Her question trembled in the air, fragile and terrifying.

Jesse swallowed hard, throat raw from salt and screaming.

"I hope so, Sadie. God, I hope so. He's tougher than any of us."

But beneath the words, fear coiled like ice. Boone had been his anchor—a brother in everything except blood.

Sadie nodded tightly, clutching the blanket like a lifeline.

The fire wrapped warmth around them inch by inch.

Then —

Down the shoreline...

Something moved.

At first Jesse thought he was seeing things. But the way it staggered, hesitated, staggered again, pulled Sadie's gaze like gravity.

A tiny shape.

Unsteady.

Dragging along.

Sadie's breath caught.

The shape limped closer.

A dog — soaked, sand-caked, trembling.

Scout.

Sadie's lips parted.

"Scout...?"

The dog stumbled, lifted her head — and saw her.

Whatever strength she had left poured into a run.

"SCOUT!!!"

Sadie tore the blanket away and fell into the sand, crawling with every ounce of strength she had left.

Her arms shook. Her knees scraped sand. Nothing mattered except reaching her.

Scout collapsed into her arms.

She gathered her close, burying her face in her wet fur. Sobs tore out of her — raw, unrestrained, the sound of something inside her snapping open.

"I thought I lost you forever... I thought I'd never see you again..."

Scout whimpered softly, pressing her muzzle into her chest. Her tail thumped twice, weak and hopeful, then rested.

She was thinner than yesterday.

She leaned her shivering weight into Sadie.

Sixteen years of trust.

Jesse dropped beside them, pulling the blanket over all three bodies. His hands shook violently, but he held the edges steady. He stroked Scout's back, voice soft and reverent.

"You're okay now, girl. You're okay."

"We're all safe."

The word all caught in his throat. Almost all.

The fisherman's wife knelt and set a small metal bowl of water in front of Scout.

"I bet you're thirsty after all you've been through," she murmured.

Scout drank desperately, water splashing onto the sand. Her whole body shook with effort.

She'd fought the same ocean they had. Alone. And she'd made it to shore.

Jesse steadied her, hand against her ribs.

"You're safe now," he whispered. "We're all safe."

The sun crested the horizon at that exact moment.

Warm.

Golden.

Impossible.

Light washed over the beach, catching on Sadie's tears, glinting on Scout's damp fur, wrapping the three of them in something soft and luminous.

Jesse lifted a trembling hand and brushed Sadie's cheek.

"I told you we'd make it," he whispered. "I wasn't sure we would... but we did."

Every stroke had felt like the last one. But he'd kept swimming because she was beside him.

Sadie pressed her forehead to his, breath catching.

"Boone... please God... let him be okay..."

Jesse smoothed a strand of hair from her face, hand unsteady but sure.

"They'll find him," he said gently. "I know they will."

Sadie searched his eyes.

"I love you, Jesse," she whispered. "I always have."

He exhaled—a soft, honest release.

"I love you too, Sadie."

Scout pushed her head between them, pressing up under their chins, insisting on belonging to this moment. Her tail tapped once beneath the blanket.

Jesse and Sadie wrapped their arms around her — around each other — around the fragile miracle of morning.

The blanket held all three of them.

Behind them, Portsmouth Island stood quiet in the morning light—the same shore that had welcomed castaways for centuries.

They were alive.

They were together.

Chapter Twenty-One

The Veil is Thin Here

The fire's warmth worked inward slowly, toward the deeper cold that still clung to their bones. The fisherman and his wife fussed over them without hesitation.

A quiet steadiness hung in the air, the kind that follows near-catastrophe.

Above them, the morning light strengthened, turning from thin pink to soft gold. The sky brightened in cautious degrees, like it was testing the world before stepping fully into it. Rays of light brushed along the sand, revealing the island in pieces: a stretch of windswept beach, faint dune lines, bits of driftwood tossed ashore like bones of old wrecks.

Portsmouth Island felt ancient. There was an emptiness to it that wasn't loneliness—more the quiet awareness of a place that had seen countless tides, countless storms, countless human stories wash through and vanish again.

Gulls flew low over the water, their wings cutting arcs in the warming air. A line of pelicans drifted in formation along the surf, breaking the smooth horizon like slow-moving shadows.

The fisherman rose from his seat, stiff in the knees but sharp in the eyes.

"Hypothermia's nothing to mess with," he said. "Y'all need to get checked out at a hospital. Want us to call the Coast Guard or the Park Service?"

His wife poured another cup of warm broth from a dented tin pot.

Sadie tightened the blanket around her shoulders. The fire had thawed the surface cold, but the deeper chill still pulsed beneath her ribs. When she spoke, her voice was softer than before, but steadier.

Her breath fogged faintly in the warming air.

"No," she said. "If we can use your cell phone... I know who to call."

The fisherman didn't hesitate. He slipped a weathered flip phone from the chest pocket of his flannel shirt and set it gently into Sadie's cold hands.

"Signal's hit-or-miss out here," he said, crouching beside the fire, "but you oughta get enough of a bar to reach who you need."

Sadie nodded, pulling the wool blanket tighter. She sat close enough to the flames that heat brushed her face in uneven waves. Jesse settled beside her in the sand, silent but steady. Scout pressed against her hip, a trembling line of warmth.

The three of them formed a small circle around the fire—exhausted, battered, but unbroken.

Sadie stared down at the phone. Her fingers shook, but she didn't pause.

She knew the number by heart.

Jesse watched her, tense but quiet.

She pressed the phone to her ear.

It rang.

Once.

Twice.

Three times.

Each ring stretched like an hour. She gripped the phone so hard her knuckles ached.

Then—

"Caleb—it's me... Sadie," she said quickly, her breath trembling.

There was a beat of stunned silence.

Then Caleb's voice came through—raw, shaking, utterly unguarded.

"Sadie? Sadie—God, is that really you? Are you okay? Where are you?"

Her breath broke with relief. Scout nudged her ribs.

Tears blurred the edges of her vision.

"Caleb... we're okay," she said. "We're alive. We're on Portsmouth. This couple—they helped us. She hesitated, fear tightening her voice. "Caleb... Boone...?"

The silence was short but sharp.

Then Caleb exhaled—a long, shaky breath.

"They found him," he said. "Coast Guard pulled him out early this morning. He's at Albemarle Hospital in Elizabeth City. He's hurt, chilled to the bone—but he's alive, Sadie. He's alive."

A sound escaped her—half sob, half laughter. Jesse bowed his head, breath trembling.

Relief washed through them like a tide finally reaching shore.

"Thank God..." Sadie whispered. "Thank God..."

"I'm already on my way to the inlet," Caleb said. "Just get there. And I'll be waiting for you."

"We'll get there," she breathed. "Caleb... thank you."

"See you soon," he said softly, and the line clicked off.

Sadie lowered the phone, breath still unsteady. Jesse leaned a little closer. Scout rested her head on her knee with a soft, weary whine.

The fisherman gave a slow, certain nod. "All right," he said gently. "Y'all don't need to be walkin' anywhere. Stay right here by this fire. I'll go get the truck and bring it 'round."

His wife adjusted the blankets around Jesse and Sadie, tucking them gently. "You stay put," she murmured. "Heat's your best friend right now."

The dry clothes the old couple had offered were more than welcome—they'd almost forgotten what comfort felt like.

The fisherman set off toward the dunes.

The fire crackled steadily. Jesse wrapped the blanket tighter around Sadie. Scout curled in her lap, muzzle tucked beneath her arm, finally resigning to sleep.

The silence that followed wasn't empty—it was comforting.

Minutes later, the fisherman's old truck appeared in a break in the dune line, sunlight flashing across its cracked windshield.

He rolled to a gentle stop near the campfire.

He leaned out the window. "All right," he called. "I've got this thing warm, let's get y'all movin'."

Jesse helped Sadie climb in slowly, still wrapped in the blanket, then lifted Scout gently into the cab and settled her across Sadie's lap. He followed. The cab smelled of sun-baked vinyl and salt.

The truck coughed twice, then rumbled to life.

The fisherman eased it into gear, and the tires churned through soft sand.

The drive was longer than Sadie expected.

They had drifted miles overnight—carried by currents, wind, and blind luck. The old truck bumped and rattled across the hard-packed sand, heater blasting, its engine groaning with every dip and rise of the shoreline.

Warm air flooded the cab. Sadie held her hands near the vent, letting the heat bleed into her fingers. Scout lay across her lap, limp with exhaustion. Jesse leaned against the back of the seat, eyes half-closed, watching the waves slide past the window.

Every breath seemed a fraction easier than the last.

The shoreline stretched for what seemed like miles.

Bleached driftwood.

Sea oats trembling in the wind.

The morning sun glinting off long arcs of surf.

The world outside the window looked newly washed—cleaned by wind and water.

Slowly—inch by inch—the world warmed around them. The storm's shadow washed away beneath sunlight and distance.

For Jesse, the teaching job in Raleigh felt like another life now. He'd made his choice.

He brushed a strand of hair from Sadie's cheek. She leaned into him.

Scout sighed, shifting gently, tail tapping once.

The fisherman's wife sat behind them, knitting needles clicking rhythmically—steady, soothing, timeless.

The warmth of the cab, the rhythm of the engine, the click of knitting needles—it all felt impossibly gentle after everything they'd survived. Sadie watched the dunes scroll past the window, but her mind was somewhere else. Somewhere beneath the water.

"Jesse," she said quietly. "There's something I need to tell you."

He turned to her, waiting.

"That night on Howard Street. The ghost tour." She paused, steadying herself. "I saw a gravestone. Set apart from the others. The lantern light caught it just as the tour was passing."

"It said Jesse Dixon. 1872-1899. Died in the line of duty. U.S. Life-Saving Service."

The name hung in the air between them.

"I asked you if anyone in your family was from here. You said your dad mentioned ancestors." She swallowed. "I didn't know what to make of it. I told myself it was coincidence."

Jesse's breath had gone shallow.

"Then, in the Life-Saving Station—the photograph. The man who looked exactly like you." Her voice trembled.

Jesse couldn't speak.

"I saw his grave before I saw his face, Jesse. He showed me. I felt it. You felt it too. He's been with us the whole time."

The truck rumbled on. Scout shifted in Sadie's lap but didn't wake.

"Last night, in the water—when I was slipping—I saw him again." Tears slid down her cheeks. "He was under the surface. Your face, but much older. It was then that I knew who he was. Your ancestor. He was speaking to me. Telling us."

"Swim to shore."

Jesse's eyes glistened.

"You said there was no shore. But he knew, Jesse. He knew it was there. He gave his life to these waters, saving strangers. And last night"—her voice broke—"he saved us."

The cab fell silent except for the engine and the soft click of knitting needles.

Then the needles stopped.

Jesse looked up. In the rearview mirror, the fisherman's eyes had found his wife's. A look passed between them—quiet, unsurprised, knowing.

The wife turned slightly, her weathered face soft with something that wasn't pity or disbelief. It was recognition.

"The veil is thin here," she said softly.

Her husband nodded once, eyes on the sand ahead. "Forty years we've been coming to this island. You learn not to question what you see... or what you feel."

The knitting needles resumed their rhythm.

Jesse reached for Sadie's hand. She laced her fingers through his.

Neither of them spoke. They didn't need to.

The ancestor who died saving strangers had reached across a century to save his own blood. And somehow, impossibly, Sadie had been the one to carry the message.

Outside, the dunes rolled past, and the morning sun painted everything in gold.

The truck curved as they passed the giant dune, revealing at last the wide, gleaming mouth of the inlet. Water shimmered beneath the rising sun.

"We're close," the fisherman said. "Reckon your friend'll be waitin' right 'round that bend."

Sadie straightened, heart thudding.

The inlet brightened before them.

A lone skiff floated near the shoreline.

A figure stood inside it—watching, scanning, waiting.

Caleb.

The moment he spotted the truck, he moved. He stepped to the bow, hand raised to his brow.

Relief crashed across his face like sunlight breaking over dark water.

Sadie gasped. Jesse exhaled sharply.

Caleb was waiting.

The fisherman rolled to a gentle stop near the tideline.

Jesse, Sadie, and Scout stepped out into warm, sunlit air.

Caleb was there.

He splashed through the shallows, water bursting around his legs. Every stride carried the fear of the night, the hope of the morning, and the overwhelming relief of seeing the people he thought he might never see again.

"Sadie! Jesse!"

His voice cracked on the shoreline.

Sadie moved first—Jesse right beside her. Scout trotted between them, gathering what strength she had left.

Caleb reached them and wrapped them both into his arms, pulling them tight.

"Thank God," he said into Sadie's shoulder. "Thank God... I thought y'all were goners."

Sadie pressed her face into his jacket. Jesse gripped the back of Caleb's neck, their foreheads nearly touching.

The embrace held all the words they didn't have breath to say.

"We're here," Jesse said softly. "We're okay."

Scout nosed Caleb's leg. Caleb knelt instantly, pulling the dog into a shaking embrace.

"You stubborn miracle," he whispered.

Scout licked his face once, exhausted but grateful.

They thanked the fisherman and his wife—quiet words carried by the morning breeze.

Sadie hugged the woman. Jesse shook the man's hand and couldn't let go.

Caleb stood, motioning toward the skiff.

"I brought blankets here in my backpack," he said. "Didn't know how cold you'd be, so I came ready."

He draped a thick wool blanket around Sadie, Jesse, and tucked a smaller one around Scout.

"Y'all ready to go to Ocracoke?" Caleb asked.

Jesse nodded. "More than ready."

Caleb steadied the skiff as Sadie stepped aboard, followed by Jesse and Scout. The boat rocked softly, warmed by sunlight.

Caleb climbed in last and pushed off from the sand.

The bow lifted into the inlet.

The same inlet that had tried to swallow them whole. Now it lay still beneath them, quiet as a held breath.

The water gleamed—sunrise stretching a widening path of gold toward Ocracoke.

Behind them, Portsmouth Island grew smaller against the horizon.

Silent. Patient. Unchanged.

Sadie leaned into Jesse. Jesse kissed the top of her head.

A small thing. But it held twelve years of silence and one night of truth.

Scout curled against their legs.

Caleb kept one hand on the wheel, but he turned often—reassuring himself they were truly there.

"You're safe now," he said. "All of you. And we're goin' home."

The skiff carried them across the bright water, the inlet opening before them like a door to another world—warm, forgiving, alive.

Boone was waiting in a hospital bed miles away. The reunion wasn't complete—not yet. But it would be.

The coast had almost killed her. But it had also given her everything. Now, she may never leave.

Wrapped in blankets, reunited at last, they crossed toward home.

Home wasn't just a place anymore. It was the people beside them. And they were already there.

The storm had ended one chapter of their lives. But as Ocracoke's harbor came into view, Sadie sensed another was just beginning.

About the author

Bobby Bryan Goodwin is a 100-ton master captain, waterman and coastal storyteller whose debut novel marks the beginning of a venture into literary fiction. Educated at the University of North Carolina at Chapel Hill, he has spent decades creating and producing regional and maritime television, including *Down East Outdoors* and *Big Rock TV*. His creative work spans novels, screenplays, television, and film, often rooted in coastal history, outdoor narratives, and the enduring pull of Southern maritime heritage.

An eighth-generation native of the Southern Outer Banks and a lifelong fisherman, he makes his home in Beaufort, North Carolina, where stories of tide, memory, and faith continue to shape his work.

www.ingramcontent.com/pod-product-compliance
Lightning Source LLC
Chambersburg PA
CBHW030912060726
47591CB00005B/1519